This novel is dedicated to you, The Reader.

Your life matters

Thank you to my friends, family, and Marines who've supported me unconditionally throughout this process.

Thank you to Jeanne Marie Leach at Novel Improvement Editorial Services for being a phenomenal writing coach and making this work come to life.

Thank you to Sally Hanan at Inksnatcher in Austin, TX for your enthusiasm in helping a young, first-time writer. I couldn't have asked for a better introduction into the writing community.

A very special thanks to some of my greatest friends, Dr. Joe Johnstone & Marine Corps Captain Austin "Indy" Quintero, for pioneering the early versions of this novel. I'll remember you both in therapy.

Silent Stag Publishers
Copyright © 2023 Anthony Jacob Acebo

ISBN-13: 979-8-9877266-0-0 (e-book)
ISBN-13: 979-8-9877266-1-7 (paperback)
ISBN-13: 979-8-9877266-2-4 (hardcover)

Cover design & graphics by: Julia Anderson at Milk & Honey Digital
Library of Congress Control Number: TXu002352579
Printed in the United States of America

Table of Contents

The Rider's Bane

Jacob Acebo

Book One

PROLOGUE

The old man walked slowly to the center of the village square and slouched onto the worn-down stump. The unfamiliar faces of travelers from the surrounding villages gathered around him, ready to hear the famous old man's final tale. The night was as cool and crisp as it had always been in the springtime, and the bright moon above cast shadows across the plain and simple village. The torchlight from the old man's audience danced across his weathered and tired face.

"This tale may be familiar to many of you," the old man muttered with a slow and raspy voice.

The crowd leaned in closer.

"I promise you that tonight it is not."

The old man let out a long sigh. "Death … is a Rider. He comes as a horseman from the abyss of the Hallowed Woods." He lifted his hand and signaled to the immense tree line behind him. "Nightmarish black as the pitch of night are he and his mare. A sturdy mount, fast and heavy in ghastly black armor. Born of the shadow from the world beyond. Atop sits the only master the beast has ever known. This is no ordinary man. Double the size of any I have ever known, even now, including those of you who stand before me. I speak of The Rider …" His voice trailed off upon speaking the name.

The old man cleared his throat.

The crowd pushed in ever closer.

"I have seen The Rider many times before. He is always peaceful to those who respect his call. For generations, his letter would appear to those due to meet death at the Hallowed Woods, precisely at midnight on the day foretold. If the traveler meets him willingly, he guides them through the Hallowed Woods and into the land beyond death." The old man clenched his fists tightly. "But this is not the tale I tell before you today. No. If this traveler were to ignore his call, The Rider would strike him down! Cold and merciless for refusing such a gift as his."

The audience watched the old man muster his strength.

"The Rider brought peace to our land. No war. No murder. Only the promise of a peaceful death. As you know, it is forbidden to step foot in the Hallowed Woods without The Rider, for the Woods do not take kindly to outsiders. No one is allowed to enter. No one."

CHAPTER 1

The Men

The cool springtime breeze blew gently through the tall trees where the young men waited. The high canopy blocked out the early morning sun, though bright hues of orange and yellow illuminated the forest enough to finally reveal their positions.

Argo leaned his back on the tree limb and slowly whittled his arrowhead into a fine point, careful not to disturb the stillness of the forest. He dragged his finger across the tip and watched as it almost punctured his skin, then slid the arrow back into the quiver lying at his side. As he readjusted his position, the tree's tough bark grazed painfully against his skin.

He peered across the dimly lit ambush sight and then up to Abaddon, who was sitting still as a stone on his tree limb. His bow lay delicately across his lap as he scanned the horizon for any sign of the beast. As he searched, he slowly turned his hunting knife in his hands. He was a large and formidable young man, even at the age of eighteen, and by far the most well built out of their group. His eyes carried the sharp and calculated gaze of a tactician which became even more apparent at times like this, in the midst of one of his carefully drawn-out plans. Though he and Argo had organized this hunt, Abaddon had taken it upon himself to be the assumed leader of the group, offering orders in the form of suggestions. His gaze shot toward Argo, as if he felt his stare. The two gave one another a subtle nod.

Castor, so skilled in archery he'd been assigned to initiate the ambush, sat on the limb beside Abaddon. Although the same age as the others, his hawkish face and boyish appearance gave him a deceptive innocence. His bow was already knocked with an arrow, and he quietly plucked his bowstring with his fingers as he waited. In all the years of their unique friendship, Argo had heard him say only a handful of words. Now he heedfully watched the forest along with Abaddon, though his attention continued to revert to Abaddon for guidance.

Argo turned behind him to check on Wander, his black and brown herding dog sitting far outside the ambush site. He could barely see her high-pointed ears poking over the large root he'd commanded her to lie behind. He raised his hand and showed her his empty palm, signaling for her to stay in place. The two of them had hunted over countless years together and had come to work seamlessly as a team. Her ears perked up at the command, then she raised her nose in the air and sniffed wildly at a new scent.

Argo searched through the high trees to see what she was picking up, but he could only smell the musty moss and dew-soaked leaves.

He turned to the limb next to him, where the last member of their group waited. Emeric, pudgy and weak, slouched lazily against the thick tree trunk. The tree limb he lay across bent and swayed under him. In his hands, he held a small block of white cheese wrapped up in a worn cloth, from which he was quietly nibbling away.

The strong and pungent scent invaded Argo's senses. He snapped to attention and hit his friend on the shoulder, signaling for him to hand over the cheese.

Emeric reluctantly passed it to him. Argo tossed it, cloth and all, into the ambush site. It landed with a thud among the fermented corn and grain the young men had lain out earlier that morning. Abaddon watched from across the site and shot Argo a look of disappointment, shaking his head in annoyed disbelief.

Argo flushed red and sank with embarrassment. For over two weeks, he and Abaddon had argued whether to bring Emeric. He was fatter and sloppier than any in their group. His family had a good number of livestock and never needed extra meat, meaning he had little to no experience hunting. Nevertheless, Argo argued that they needed the extra bow, and he wouldn't be an issue as long as he could shoot sitting from a limb, which was easy enough. Now Argo was beginning to doubt his decision. He felt an overwhelming sense of guilt for pushing the idea so hard. If anything happened to Emeric, he would be responsible.

Argo braced himself on his limb and leaned in close to Emeric. "We went over this. No food. Can't have any unnatural scent," he told him in a low whisper. "Abaddon and I have been tracking this great boar for over two weeks now. You said you wanted a chance to come, and I vouched for you."

Emeric tightened his lips and nodded shamefully in agreement. He repositioned himself to straighten out his posture, then grabbed his bow and rested it in his lap like the others.

Argo raised his hand to shield his eyes from the first rays of morning sunlight breaking through the forest canopy. Far beneath them, a beautiful array of colors illuminated the mossy and root-laden ground. The trees were tall and slender and blooming with the vibrant green of a fresh spring season. A quiet stillness lay between the group of friends, which under most circumstances would be comforting, but in this moment was filled with a certain uneasiness. They were waiting to ambush a great boar that was easily twice, if not three times, the size of normal boars. Its massive tusks could easily cut through a man if he wasn't careful.

Argo looked at his friends with concern. He and Abaddon were experienced hunters and could hold their own. Castor, though quiet, could be relied upon to hold a steady shot and react professionally to most situations. Emeric, however, was untested and could jeopardize the whole operation. Their village had already expressed their disapproval for the hunt, saying it was too dangerous and wasteful of a Rider's gift. If something went wrong, it would surely mean the end of great boar hunts. They would rather have the young men safely hunt rabbits or squirrels than a beast who could fight back. As they waited, Argo thought through the considerations—

The foul smell of Emeric's cheese was replaced by a pungent odor caught in the breeze. He winced at it, recognizing the smell. Emerging through the distant trees came the great boar, even larger than he remembered. The beast caught the scent of the cheese and fermented corn and grunted loudly as he searched it out.

Argo signaled to Abaddon, who'd already been watching the beast, then slowly leaned back to Emeric again and patted him on the shoulder, pointing in the boar's direction. Emeric jolted upright at the sight and clumsily readied his bow.

The young men remained fixed on the beast as it lumbered straight to the bait. His thick snout dug relentlessly through the dirt, and he tore up the soil with tusks the size of human arms, grunting and snorting loudly as he ate. The long-awaited moment had come, and the young men carefully drew their bows to a full draw.

Emeric's hands shook wildly as he held the animal in his sights. Even Argo felt his fingers begin to sweat from his firm hold. The tight bow string dug deeply into his fingers under the tension. They watched until the great boar seemed comfortably indulged in his meal, then Abaddon gave a subtle nod.

Castor made a knocking sound with his mouth. The boar looked up, exposing the prime target area of his chest. Without hesitation, Castor released his arrow, which struck powerfully into the chest of the beast. Suddenly, three more arrows whistled through the air and thudded loudly into the lungs and shoulders of the boar, who wailed an ear-shattering cry and bucked wildly into the air. The ground shook violently like an earthquake when he landed.

The branch holding Emeric broke from the tree with a tremendous crack and sent him crashing to the forest floor. His large, thick body hit the ground aggressively, drawing the attention of their prey. The beast kicked once more into the air and thrashed his head angrily.

Argo's tree limb shook from the beast bucking. He braced himself in case his branch broke too.

Emeric held his leg with one arm and clawed desperately with the other for his bow laying a distance from him—then cried out as the boar charged toward him.

Argo dropped from his branch and held onto it, then jumped to the forest floor. The impact stung his heels and buckled his knees, sending him flat to the ground.

The boar grunted loudly and barreled toward Emeric.

Scrambling to get up, Argo quickly knocked another arrow and struck the beast behind the front shoulder mid-stride.

The boar tumbled loudly and broke off several of the arrows in the process, leaving the tips still buried in his side.

"Wander!" Argo cried to his dog.

Wander sprang instantly, with an unimaginable speed from her position outside the ambush, directly toward the beast's hind legs. Throwing herself recklessly at the great boar, she sank her teeth into his shin, then thrashed furiously and pulled backward with all her weight to hold the great creature in place.

The young men shot more arrows that sank sharply into the boar's chest like a pin cushion. The beast cried out again, tossing and turning destructively in revolt of his attackers. Wander desperately held on, but with a swift kick, the beast threw her off. She flew through the forest and rolled across the large roots.

The beast regained himself and sighted Argo, who for a moment froze in terror. The great boar lowered his head and charged.

Argo's hands shook as he let loose another arrow which missed entirely.

Emeric screamed in pain.

The wild animal paid no attention.

Argo desperately ran in the opposite direction from Emeric and took cover behind a nearby tree. He drew the small blade from his waistband and readied himself as the beast raced toward him. "Shoot him!" he cried loudly to his friends.

Above him, Abaddon and Castor loosed two more arrows that struck the beast's neck and upper spine dropping the animal dead in its tracks. The suddenly lifeless mass slid across the forest floor and slammed into the tree shielding Argo.

Silence fell over them.

Staying behind the tree, Argo drew his bow again and fixed it on the beast. His chest rose laboriously and then it stopped. No one dared move until they were sure he wouldn't spring back to life. Wander cautiously approached the great boar and ran her nose around him. Then she ran happily to Argo, who lowered his bow and embraced her. Her tail wagged as she greeted him, and then she ran back and studied the foe.

Argo ran over to Emeric, who sat grasping his leg tightly.

Abaddon and Castor climbed down from their tree and met up with them.

Emeric lifted his hands and stared at the hole in his thigh, wanting to scream again. A small stump from the downed tree limb had stabbed Emeric's thigh when he fell, and the wound was now leaking steadily with dark, crimson blood.

Argo did his best to calm him down. He moved his friend's hands and placed his own over the wound. Fortunately, he'd seen accidents before, and he knew he needed to stop the bleeding. The dark, warm blood seeped through his fingers.

Abaddon took off his cloak and gave it to Argo. "Here, use this," he said strongly. Argo pressed it against the wound, and the blue cloak soaked into a dark purple. The wound was deep, but not deep enough to be fatal. However, they were concerned about the possibility of infection setting in. They'd known villagers of the past who received an early letter from The Rider from similar infections.

When the bleeding slowed down, they carefully pulled the cloak away. The dried blood crusted around the wound and stuck to the fabric.

"You'll be fine," Argo reassured him. "The bleeding stopped." He patted one hand on his back.

Abaddon tied the cloak tightly around the wound and got Emeric back on his feet. They carried him closer to the great boar and set him back down against a tree nearby. The young men gathered around and studied the massive beast, who smelled of sweaty dirt and waste. Trails of dried blood formed around the arrows pinned in his hide. The dark and dirty fur was still warm to the touch.

In times after a hunt, Argo's hands uncontrollably shook from the excitement, as if the shock of it all were catching up to him at once. He felt relief, but when he thought of jumping down to the boar's level and placing himself in danger, he also felt something else, a euphoric thrill he'd never felt before in his life.

The young men set to cleaning the kill. They struggled to pull the great boar away from the tree and remove the numerous arrows in his side. Despite the task, Argo couldn't lose his thoughts about how bravery such as his act today was rare, particularly since The Rider had begun leading the dead to the afterlife. Without a doubt, the village would be upset if they heard about it.

Any tales of bravery were from a time long before Argo's generation. Those stories were of only one hero, The Great Hero Adonillis, an ancient warrior of a thousand battles. In the stories, he stood taller than any man and rode a great and powerful horse that came to his aid at the blow of a whistle, no matter the distance. Arrows bounced off his armor, and he could dodge any spear or swinging sword. He always won. He never lost. He was, in fact, the only hero in any tale."

Emeric sat by himself against the tree and rubbed his hands over his wound. He winced and breathed loudly at the pain.

The young men didn't speak a word. They pulled back the hide of the great boar, and Abaddon glided his knife across the membrane holding it to the meat. It cut smooth and effortlessly through the soft tissue. "How's your leg doing, Emeric?" he asked, finally breaking the silence.

"It'll be fine. My mother's going to hate me for this though," he answered with a shameful tone.

"Well, you could've been killed," Abaddon retorted. "The village hasn't had a natural death in ages, and here you are trying your damnedest to be the first. The Rider's gift means we have a promised, peaceful death if we don't kill ourselves before receiving our letter. And Argo, your want of bravery is so strong that you crossed into recklessness to find it." He stopped cleaning the boar's skin with his sharp knife and pointed it at both of them. "Mark my words, if one of us gets killed out here, that'll be the last time the village allows us to hunt great boar. Then it'll be squirrels and rabbits 'til the end of our days. We can't mention any of this when we get back, all right?" Then he added in a quiet tone, "Don't throw away the gift of The Rider."

Argo made no attempt to refute, only nodded and said, "You're right." His friends all knew where he stood, Abaddon even more so, who spoke an unfortunate truth that Argo hated to hear.

"I'm sorry, guys," Emeric responded, "I should've been more careful. It's my first time doing something like this, and I messed it up."

"It's all right, Emeric," Abaddon replied. "Just be more careful next time. You know how I get about this." He had an impeccable ability to unite groups, and while it had always felt genuine, Argo thought it was out of a sense of fear that something might go wrong. As if the group were a herd of sheep that would drive itself off a cliff if not for their duly appointed shepherd. Argo both appreciated and resented Abaddon's ability to bring people together. Despite his love for his friends and family, Argo felt as if he existed in the space outside that herd. A black sheep unable to be herded, yet one who stuck around for the company. Perhaps this quality was what drew Abaddon to him as a peer instead of a leader; that somehow Argo was unconquerable. Perhaps this clash of personalities was what formed a deeper friendship between them.

The young men fell back into silence as they worked on the great boar, which was no easy task given the size. Castor fetched the wheelbarrow they'd positioned at the edge of the Woods.

Argo broke off a hoof and gave it to Wander, who lay down beside him and became entranced with her meal.

The group carefully cut the meat and chucked it in the wheelbarrow.

"Did any of you stay up and watch The Rider last night?" Abaddon asked them.

"No," Emeric and Argo both said.

"Castor?" Abaddon asked.

Castor shook his head silently.

"What was the lady's name?" Argo asked to keep the conversation going.

They looked at one another and shrugged their shoulders.

"Not sure. Does it matter? She was from one of the Northern villages though, not one of our own," Abaddon replied. "I saw it. Couldn't sleep, so I went out to the square and watched from a distance. Terrifying, The Rider."

"What do you think happens when he takes them into the Woods?" Emeric asked.

"I'm sure Argo knows, after all those tales the Lady's told him. Isn't that right, Argo?" Abaddon asked sarcastically.

Argo had, in fact, frequently visited the Lady of the Woods. He was going to do so once more after this hunt since she lived in the same forest—to the east of their village—where they hunted. She was a mystic and mysterious woman unlike any Argo had ever met, full of stories and tales from far-off lands which infamously made her an outcast from those in their village. Though she never refused to host visitors as they traveled west to meet with The Rider.

"That's right. I know all about it. Maybe when you all stop being so scared, you can ask the Lady yourself," he answered with just as much sarcasm as Abaddon.

"Well, my mother says that everyone in the village says to stay away from her," Emeric replied. "They say she spreads lies and ideas that get people in trouble."

"And who are *they*, the ones who say such things?" Argo asked, not so jokingly anymore. "Anybody could be *they*. Even me."

"Look," Abaddon butted in, "I was just poking fun at you, Argo. We've already run this into the ground. I just worry about you spending too much time with her. You've been different ever since you started visiting her."

"Different? What do you mean?" Argo asked defensively.

Castor and Emeric passed each other an awkward glance.

"You know what I mean, Argo. Jumping down over a wild great boar? Why would you do that?" Abaddon stopped shearing the meat and played with the knife in his hand.

"He was charging Emeric," he answered. "I had to."

"It was still reckless. There were other options. We could've shot him from the safety of the trees. You just chose the storybook option." Abaddon's voice rose and became sharper.

"A thousand things could've happened," Argo said, meeting his tone. "But only one did. Besides, there wasn't much time to think through all of them."

The two going back and forth like this was a hallmark of their long friendship. Argo was the only one Abaddon ever allowed to speak to him like this. Argo slid his knife through the meat, then sat back on his heels. "Maybe I did it because I'm trying to find more to life than this … I don't know … this waiting game we're playing. I feel like all we're doing is just waiting for our letter to go die." He threw some more meat into the wheelbarrow.

"You're letting those stories get to you. They're stories, Argo. They're made up. Not real life," Abaddon explained. "You're always trying to play the hero like you're The Great Hero Adonillis."

"Well," Argo answered, then thought for a second. "Maybe they can happen in real life. Maybe I did it because that's who I want to be."

"Yeah, well, we're your friends and we care about you. You blur the lines between your dreams and real life. Also if anything happens to you, I'm going to be left with Castor for conversation," Abaddon joked.

Castor looked up and gave no response, surprising no one.

"To answer your question, Emeric," Abaddon said, quickly changing the subject, "we know what happens. The travelers go with The Rider into the Hallowed Woods and move peacefully to the world beyond. That's all there is to know."

Abaddon tossed another one of the cleaned bones to Wander, who watched it hit the ground in front of her. She stared at it, then went back to chewing the hoof, unsure of which one to go for.

At least she understands how I feel.

Abaddon removed the long tusks and studied them carefully. He ran his bloodied hands across the rugged surface, which smelled of a strange and wild scent. The tusks were covered from top to bottom in long scratches and scars. One of them was broken at the tip and had a thick, open crack riding down its side.

"Look at this," he said, motioning his group over. "Remember when we first saw this guy a couple of weeks ago?" He handed the broken tusk to Argo. "I was hoping I'd see this up close. Without it stabbing through me of course."

As Argo admired the tusk, his stomach felt queasy, almost to the point of throwing it to the ground. And yet he also admired the tusk, running his hands across it. Abaddon had left his bloody fingerprints on it. The dark crimson marking contrasted brightly against the ivory. The sheer immensity of the situation threatened his stomach again. Thoughts of the tusk tearing through him flashed across his mind, and he felt both foolish and incredibly lucky that he was unharmed. "I don't want it," Argo said, handing it back to Abaddon. "Makes me think of what could've happened."

"Maybe you should keep it then," he replied, taking it back. "Price of being a hero."

The response annoyed Argo. Though Abaddon had always maintained a distaste for recklessness, Argo liked to believe that some part of him secretly envied it, which could be the reason why they'd always been best friends. "You should come with me to see the Lady," he said. "Could be good for you. I'm going there from here."

"I'd rather carry cheese boy back than see her," Abaddon said. "You should be careful though. She's changing you."

"She is," Argo agreed. "But caterpillars change into butterflies. Doesn't mean that's bad."

Abaddon smirked. "That sounds like something she'd say." There was something strangely defiant in his tone, as if it were a matter of principle for him rather than reason.

The young men helped Emeric stand on his good leg and propped him next to Abaddon, who winced at his weight. Behind them, Castor struggled with the wheelbarrow as Argo stood and watched the group set off to the west and their humble, quiet village. He wrapped his scraps of meat in a cloth and headed farther east to visit the Lady of the Woods. Seeing her was always the highlight of his day. She was the only one who truly resonated with him, who he could explore ideas and speak freely with. The uneasy feeling in his stomach lightened, and he felt recomposed again.

Wander followed closely behind and wagged her tail merrily, a bone gripped tightly in her mouth.

CHAPTER 2

The Lady

Overgrown roots wove across the footpath to the main road. Argo and Wander reached it in no time and headed east, away from their village. The road was frequently traveled by wagons and livestock from the surrounding villages, but the road was most notably known as the "Travelers' Way," due to it being the main road for those meeting with The Rider.

The sun was almost at midday when the two reached the long pathway leading to the Lady's home, which was marked with a small wooden sign painted on both sides with colorful wildflowers. It contained no words, yet everyone in the land knew its meaning. Wander sprang forward with excitement when she recognized it.

Her home was concealed out of sight from the main road behind several tall trees. At the start of the path near the sign, the Lady had planted thin trees along both sides of the footpath and fashioned them into an archway, which over time had grown intricate and beautiful, with vines and flowers adding to the mysterious divinity.

They passed under the archway and through a rich sea of wildflowers that had grown as high as Wander. Then the path opened to a clearing in the forest with a weathered wooden fence around an old-yet-pristine cabin overgrown with vibrant green vines. Surrounding the home, a vast garden of vegetables, herbs, and trees of all shapes and sizes flourished in an organized fashion. Rich smells of cinnamon, spices, and unknown foreign scents drifted through the air, invigorating the senses of each traveler.

If only the guys could see this. Then they might change their minds.

Wander ran to the front door and waited impatiently while Argo set down the cloth full of meat. It thudded against the wood decking underneath. He looked at Wander and knocked.

"Back here!" the Lady called from behind the cabin.

Wander darted to the sound of her voice. Argo picked up the meat and followed. Behind the cabin he saw Wander nearly on top of the Lady, licking away at her face. She laughed and gave Wander kisses, then a big hug. She was working in her garden and covered head to toe in dirt and sweat. Despite this, she held an indescribable beauty, which could only be described as ethereal, divine, or out of this world. Her energy was old and motherly, yet she appeared in her early thirties. She was skinny and thin, and had long brown hair with hints of red throughout. Her skin was a dark tan and covered in freckles from her long hours working in the sun. She was kind and warm, and she spoke in a way that made everything seem grand and interesting.

"Argo! Come here. Look at this." The Lady signaled him over, her hand delicately extended to the dirt. Nestled in her soft grasp was a blue wildflower.

"Look at this flower." She motioned for him to come closer. "This single flower is particularly special to me. You see?"

He reached down and studied it closely between his fingers. His eyes widened, and he peered closer. The Lady watched him. The petals were simple and inelegant, yet they glowed mysteriously with a brilliant-blue fluorescent light unlike any he'd seen before. He leaned in closer and smelled a lavish assortment of sweet and mysterious fragrances.

"I've never seen anything like it. The color..." He peered at it deeply and ran his thumb across one of the petals. "It has its own light ... What is it?"

"It has many names, but I call it the Blue Hue." She leaned down beside Argo and took the flower back in her hand. She peered deeply into it as she spoke. "Now, this single flower is very particular, and not only in its color, you see? It has to be planted along with many others deep in the soil on the first day of winter. Now, you can plant it in the spring along with the other flowers in the garden, but once it grows, the petals will just be a normal blue, not fluorescent like this, and it will look indistinguishable from all the other flowers in the garden. What makes this single flower special is that when it's planted among the others in winter, only one endures to blossom."

She looked at Argo to make sure he was following. He nodded, silently encouraging her to continue.

"You see," she said, "when they're forced to endure the hardship of a long and cold winter, they pull together all their resources for this one seed." She looked back at the flower in her hand. "The only one to blossom."

Argo looked deeply into the center of the flower. Its beauty radiated forth from its core, as if it grew seamlessly from the soil and into his soul.

"You see, when I look at these plants in my garden, I recognize how easy it is to take this all for granted. And when I see this single flower here, what do I know of the troubles it endured? And the life of the many other seedlings to produce such a creation? To us, it's just another beautiful flower." Her words drifted to a comfortable silence between them.

Wander reached to sniff the flower and then sneezed. Argo thought back to the hunt that morning. Memories of the boar charging him flashed in his mind, and his heart quickened. "I guess the same could be said about the great boar that we killed this morning," he responded.

"Yes! Exactly." The Lady smiled and acknowledged the cloth full of great boar meat.

Argo smiled back and paused for a moment. "I kind of feel bad about him when you put it that way," he said half-jokingly.

"Don't feel bad, Argo," she reassured him as she let go of the flower, careful not to pull it from the ground. "Such is the way of life."

"Well, not for us," Argo said in an almost guilty tone. He didn't look at her but instead gestured toward the surrounding flowers in her garden, then shrugged his shoulders. "What do we know about his life or about the way he lived and what he did to get there? Sometimes while hunting or cleaning the kill, I've thought about that—how terrifying it must be to be hunted, and about the courage it takes for them to fight back."

"M'hm," the Lady nodded in agreement. Her short response reeled more out of him.

"Why is death given to us so warmly while it's dealt so coldly to others?"

The Lady had a way of calling forward his deepest thoughts, which constantly drew Argo back to her. No one in his village entertained conversations like this.

"Don't you see, Argo?" She looked at him, then back to the single flower. "It's difficult to fully appreciate this world and all it endures. It may not seem like it, but this world is full of great courage and great love, though not all these tales are told. It's ingrained in the cycle of life. Bravery is not just for The Great Hero Adonillis. It's in everything and everyone, in the small actions we take just to make it one more day, just like these seedlings who sacrificed themselves for this single flower."

The three admired the flower glowing softly in the sunlight.

"All of that hard work for this flower," he said softly as he stared into its center. It danced lightly in the wind. "And for what? What does it become?" Argo asked.

She plucked the flower from the dirt. "It becomes rather great tea."

CHAPTER 3

The Tea

The two sat at their usual places at the Lady's kitchen table and shared their tea, which tasted and smelled every bit as amazing as she'd claimed. The steeping flower petals filled the house with a sweet and earthy scent. When she poured it in their teacups, it gave off a slight neon-blue light, as if it captured the moonlight.

Wander slept at their feet, with her body stretching out to touch both of them.

Argo told her of the hunt and of Emeric's injuries and how his friends addressed how reckless he was to have jumped down to face the beast. He had a habit of telling his own tales in the same manner the Lady told him tales of The Great Hero Adonillis, yet he also had the habit of dismissing each action. "It was reckless," he would say, or "I should have been more careful."

The Lady of the Woods listened intently. She leaned in from her chair at the exciting parts and leaned back during his reflections. She made no interruptions and listened to the story from beginning to end, nodding and gasping when appropriate.

As he spoke, he played with the flower petals floating gently in his cup. The entrancing glow made it easier to recall the day's events. When he finished the tale, the Lady rested back into her chair and slowly nodded her head without saying a word. She swirled the tea in her cup and took another sip as the story resonated in the silence between them. "Incredible," she finally said. "You know, Argo, The Great Hero Adonillis had friends too. None of them made their way into the tales that I've told you. None but his horse. Have you noticed that?"

"No." Argo shook his head. "I guess I've never really noticed. Why's that?"

"Well, one, because they were never told to me either," she joked. "And two, and this is just my opinion of course, is that they may have been similar to your friends. I like to imagine that Adonillis had many friends and even family, all whom he held dear and close. And remember, this was before The Rider. This was when death was real. Perhaps they cared for him just as dearly, and perhaps, even after his thousandth battle, they still held the same fear in their heart that the next would be the one when they would lose their friend." She set her teacup down on the table between them. "You understand the pain of loss."

Argo thought of his mother, who'd traveled with The Rider several years prior. Though her passing had been as peaceful as it could be, he still harbored pain in his heart and missed her dearly. No words or comfort from his friends could fill the void left by her passing. "I do," Argo admitted, still toying with the petal in his teacup. "I still think about my mother every day."

"M'hm," the Lady agreed. "It's not easy letting go, nor saying goodbye, even if the time is given to us. Perhaps your friends, and Adonillis' friends for that matter, value your presence more than your ambitions. Relationships can be like a scale, you see." She put her open hand out over the table. "On one hand, you have your friends or family or whoever." She opened her other hand. "On the other hand, you have yourself. Too much of their wants and desires upset the balance and take away from you. Too much of your own wants and desires can take away from them, upsetting the balance as well. What you must decide is where you're willing to give and where you're willing to take."

Argo leaned back in silence and let the Lady's words sink in. He reached down from his chair and scratched Wander behind her ears while he reflected. She lay still in her sleep. Her tongue stuck slightly out of her mouth which always gave Argo a little laugh when he saw it. "I can see that," he finally replied. He let the words fill the air and resonate, then die down. "It's hard dealing with loss. I can see why people avoid it. If my mother was being reckless, I'm sure I would've been the same way toward her that my friends are toward me."

"M'hm," she replied. "I'm sure we all would."

"It's an interesting problem, death," he said. "It's ultimately inevitable for all of us, yet it's so difficult to come to grips with. There's never a good time. Not now, not even when we're old and gray. It always comes too soon, no matter how late." Argo's mind was hard at work, grinding and turning the gears to process his raw idea into conveyable words. He looked at the Lady as she silently took another sip of tea. Her silence pulled more out of him.

"I understand why my friends were upset. I would've felt the same if I'd lost one of them in the same way … It can be frustrating at times. How can we do anything great if we're always so careful? And careful of what?" he asked. "We all know what's ultimately going to happen to us. It makes no difference to anyone but me if I was to have walked or run here, but it makes all the difference in the world how I choose to arrive at my own death."

The Lady set her empty glass of tea on the table. "Sometimes, Argo—" she leaned in closer "—death is only real to the ones it leaves behind."

CHAPTER 4

The Father

The walks home from visiting the Lady had never failed to rejuvenate Argo. He had time to reflect on the lessons he'd learned and relate them to his own life. Oftentimes, after hearing stories of The Great Hero Adonillis, he'd pick up large sticks and pretend they were swords. He'd imagine fighting groups of enemies just like in the tales. When he was sure no one was watching, he'd swing the great stick and knock it against the trees, skillfully maneuvering in and out of them. When Wander would play along and bite the stick, he'd dance around her and pull it away when she reached for it.

Not today.

Today, his thoughts retraced the Lady's words. He replayed the conversation over and over again in his mind, making sure to absorb every bit of it. "Maybe that's what makes a great friend," he said out loud to Wander. "Someone who leaves you with a new perspective. Not one that's forced, but one gently presented, to discover and explore on your own. Also, someone who just listens to you spill ideas and then helps piece them together once they're out."

Wander kept walking and shook her tail even more now that he was talking to her.

Reciting his thoughts out loud to Wander had always given him comfort. She'd always been a great listener and rarely ever interrupted his train of thought. Speaking his ideas out loud helped make his thoughts real. It gave his words weight and structure. Once they were spoken, he could almost piece them together like pieces of a puzzle. Despite Wander being a dog, she felt more human than anyone he knew.

He thought back to the Lady's comments on appreciation and noticed the vines overtaking the trees, and how the roots below him meshed together into thick, wise trunks that rose separately out of the ground and meshed again at the top. He noticed the birds singing in the distance.

"What hardships have these birds endured to produce such songs?" he asked aloud again. "What do they have to sing so merrily about?"

The Lady's presence was a breath of fresh air in a colorless and dull world. *If there's any good left in the world, that's what it looks like.* This wasn't in a romantic way but in a way that made him feel alive, like the feeling of a fresh bath or a hot tea in the morning. She bettered him. She bettered his thinking and his attitude toward the world. She was a lens that saw the world differently, perhaps from another angle or in another light. His friends would never understand, though he secretly hoped they at least viewed him in the same respectful light as he viewed the Lady.

Abaddon's words still rang in his head, and Argo knew them to be true—he had changed. He was no longer the young boy who first stumbled upon her forest home years ago. He'd grown into something different now, evolved, sharpened. The Lady was a whetstone who honed his mind and thought process with each meeting. He had begun to see the world through the same lens as her.

The sun tucked itself away behind the horizon as the two reached the opening of the trail, broke through the clearing of the forest, and once again came in sight of their village. Orange hues of sunlight rose from the tall trees of the Hallowed Forest behind the buildings. Though the sun did not truly set for another hour, the massive height of the trees blocked the sun well before it actually fell behind the horizon.

As they approached their home, Wander sprinted forward toward the front porch and jumped on Argo's father, who would normally sit in his large wooden chair and smoke his pipe. This time he stood and leaned with his back against the small home. He was a large, burly man with a thick, unkempt beard. His sleeves were rolled to his elbows as usual, and he crossed his arms tightly against his chest. He never appeared too joyful, not since Argo's mother had traveled with The Rider years ago. Now he wore a deeply concerned look in his eyes that gave a silent and piercing glare. Tightly clenched in his hand, he held a slip of old parchment folded into a letter. As if he lacked the strength to deliver a single word himself, his father held it out for Argo. His hand struggled to hold it steady.

Although they never spoke about it, Argo knew his father had desperately wanted his letter. He missed his wife more than anything in the world. Argo looked in his eyes and took the letter. His hands were surprisingly calm since he knew it was for his father, though the look in his eyes concerned him.

The old letter was folded three times over on thick, tan parchment. A circular seal of black wax had once held it together but was now split in half. There were no insignias or formalities of any kind. He ran his thumb across the cold wax seal and looked back at his father, who gave a slight nod then looked away.

Argo opened it and dropped it to the ground. On the wooden deck lay the open letter that simply said:

ARGO

6 DAYS HENCE

CHAPTER 5

The Letter

A dark night swept quickly over the quiet village. Only the stars and candlelit cabin windows illuminated the outside. Crickets played their songs over the rustling of wind through the garden. Their home had always been small, yet tonight the walls were closer than ever before. It had always been a simple home for a simple family. Argo and his father sat silently around the hearth while Wander lay at her master's feet. Argo sat hunched over her with his head in his hands, his nerves shaking uncontrollably. When he looked up, he saw his father quickly look away from him and get up to stand closer to the fire.

He'd always regarded his father as a dreary man, though Argo had heard stories from his mother about how lively he'd been in his youth. However, once she'd received her letter and traveled with The Rider, that spark seemed to have traveled as well. Now his days consisted of tending the crops and the few livestock they had, day in and day out. The thick calluses in his hands told of the many hours he toiled away on chores to fill the void he harbored.

Argo fixed himself upright in his plain wooden chair and watched his father. The man now leaned up against the side of the cabin, entranced by the fire of the hearth. His eyes were swollen with grief, though he maintained a desperate and honest attempt to remain stoic on the outside. He puffed away at his pipe, and the smoke drifted gently up and out of the window he stood beside. The more he puffed, the more Argo understood the smoldering ember burning deep within his father. He had wanted that letter to be for him.

No father should have to see his son go before his time. The gravity of loneliness from Argo traveling with The Rider would be too much for him to bear. His wife had been taken only a few years back, and the home had undeniably never been the same. She was a bright soul, though stoic in her own ways as well. Her grace and beauty weren't meant for this world, and maybe that's what his father saw in her.

Argo stared into the hearth, wondering how he should feel. He felt odd. He didn't feel stricken with grief, nor necessarily scared, but anxious more than anything. He played with the letter in his hands and unfolded it once more.

ARGO

6 DAYS HENCE

Is this it? He flipped the letter over and held it against the light of the fire. The light shined right through it, revealing no other sign or indication of its message.

Not even any instructions?

He ran his fingers softly across the ink and thought back to his mother's letter, but he couldn't remember any details. She'd reacted so casually to the matter that he hadn't thought much of it in his young age. He folded the letter and sat back in his chair, then looked at his family's sword mounted above the fireplace. It had been mounted there and untouched all his life. It had once been used in the times before The Rider, but now it sat in its sheath, never to be drawn again.

How is anyone supposed to feel when confronted with such an unstoppable force bestowed upon them? Is it going to hurt? Will it be bloody? Will The Rider and I casually walk through the Woods until we eventually reach the other side? Should I bring supplies? Something to sleep on? Something to keep warm at night? Water? Why have I never bothered to ask this before?

Each question crafted another stream of unanswered concerns. Amidst the whirlwind of thoughts, he saw himself as another traveler in a long line of travelers, one whose number was called, the same as those before him. That had been the nature of life and death for all the time he'd known, except for the tales he'd heard of The Great Hero Adonillis.

He held the letter so tightly in the grip of his fingers that sweat from his grasp lightly soaked through it. He thought back to the morning when they'd received his mother's letter. She had only been given one day's notice before her meeting with The Rider. The three of them sat on their front porch the entire day, and around the warm hearth once night fell, exchanging stories and love and laughs. Wander had been no older than a puppy at the time, and she'd lain on her back on his mother's lap, begging for her belly to be rubbed the whole day.

His mother had never once shown how scared she was, or if she had been, she'd done an excellent job of hiding it. He was proud of her for how she acted that night. At midnight that night, they and many others in the village gathered to watch her stand at the edge of the tree line and greet The Rider, strangely, like an old friend. Both he and his father were crying, and Argo had to keep a rope around Wander to keep her from following his mother.

Argo, his family, and others in the village had seen The Rider many times before his mother's letter. He always arrived precisely at midnight, riding tall on his armor-clad warhorse and appearing exactly how Abaddon had described him. The horseman would peacefully ride out of the Woods of the Abyss and, without words, circle the traveler once and then walk them back into the forest. It had always been a solemn and uncelebrated event.

Argo had heard tales of the village performing rituals and ceremonies on the night of a traveler's journey, but somewhere along the years, those rituals had ceased, and now only some of the village folk gathered to see them off. The only resemblance of some sort of care came from acts like a small knapsack of keepsakes, or baked treats and bread, that the family would give to the traveler so that they could remember them in the next world.

Argo had given his mother a small wooden arrowhead that he'd carved out of wood. It wasn't much, but he'd put many hours into carving it. He'd taken out his knife and carefully whittled away the wood to create an even sharper and finer point. He had no intention of giving it away, but as the circumstance demanded, it was all he had to give that his parents hadn't given him themselves. When he gave it to her, she gave a big, astonished smile and hugged Argo, thanking him for the greatest gift ever. He would never forget how she'd made him feel.

Argo's father coughed loudly and broke the silence, almost choking. "It's a gift," he muttered quietly. Smoke billowed out of his pipe, and he exhaled it in a long and steady breath. "They say that he removes the pain of death. Not for me, I say. I feel its pain every day. Sometimes it's all I feel. But when I see you, my only child, I don't feel it so much." Another tear rolled down his cheek and vanished behind his beard. "If I had the courage of the hero in your tales, I would ask The Rider to take me and be done with it—"

"I'm tired of hearing about Adonillis," Argo said. "Tired of it. I'm tired of the endless tales while we just waste away here. Are we not good enough to have tales of our own?" The words came pouring out of him. He realized this outburst and pulled himself back into his chair. "I'm sorry, Father." He looked back at the fire, ashamed to face the man. "I feel the same way about mother passing." He looked back at his surviving parent. "I'm tired of this world. If there is something after all of this, I hope it's … more." His words faded off.

His father said nothing and stared into the fire. His arms were still crossed over his chest.

"What's the point?" Argo whispered under his breath. He shook his head and stood up, resting his back against the wall next to him. "We waste our time until our name is beckoned, and then we go, and the world carries on without us the same as it did before we were here. And what of us? What of those who travel with The Rider, like Mother? They live in our memories until we pass as well, and so goes the cycle until there's no memory left to pass down. I agree, Father. I agree with everything you say. And now that it's my name called, I don't know how I feel. I want to feel angry, but that's not right. Sad maybe? Sad that my time has come and I've done nothing in this world. The memory of me won't live long past my time." Argo peered deeply into the flames, searching for an answer.

His father ran his hand over his dark beard and looked deeply at his child. "I know it isn't much, my son, but I'll never let go of your memory. Nor your mother. Wherever she may be, I know she remembers you every moment of the day. We can never let you be forgotten in this world or the next. You must understand that." He moved over and placed his hand on Argo's shoulder. He'd never shown affection toward him, and now it seemed almost awkward, but he could feel the sincerity. His hand rested there with a strange and unique weight.

"Thanks, Father."

"It isn't right, son. None of it is." He took his hand off Argo's shoulder and folded his arms once again. "But I think of times like this and am thankful for what we have. What else is there to think about? I don't have to worry about a gruesome, unexpected death like we've heard of from the times before The Rider. As much as I miss your mother, I'm thankful that she didn't suffer. I suppose that's the best we could really hope for. At least, that's what I tell myself."

Argo nodded slowly. The light of the flame danced wildly around the room as his eyes peered deeply in its motion. His mind raced like a trapped great boar from the morning's hunt. He clenched his fists and looked down at the letter in his hand. It crumpled under his grip.

"No," he said quietly under his breath. He shook his head and looked into the fire. "I'm going to go into the Hallowed Woods, and I'm going to meet The Rider myself."

CHAPTER 6

The Plan

Argo's will was set, and a fire brighter than any hearth raged in his eyes.

His father let out a long sigh and looked to the ground, almost wanting to smile at the joke. His eyes met with Argo's, and he understood the severity of his statement. "Son, no, no." He shook his head and almost laughed. "Is this because of what I was saying? Did I give you this stupid idea?"

"No, I've always thought about doing it. I just never mentioned it to anyone," he replied.

"No. Nobody goes into the Hallowed Woods without The Rider." He stood up straight from the wall. "That's how it is, and that's how it always will be. The village would never allow it. You're blessed with a gift, son. Use it. It's so close for you. We pay our dues, and when our time is called, we answer. That's how it works. It worked for you mother; it will work for you, and it will work for me." His words quickened. With each line, he pointed with the wooden pipe in his hand. "You're young and don't understand."

"No, I understand, Father," Argo said as he stood up as well. "What's the point of all of this? To just waste our time in the hopes of something better?" Argo met his father's eyes for a moment, then quickly looked into the fire again. "If it is so, and that's all we're meant for, then I mean to change it. Who says the heroic stories are just for Adonillis and people we've never met? Who's to say that they even existed to begin with?"

"Son, don't let your ambition blind your judgment. I understand. The news of this can't be easy, but you need to think this through. I was always worried about you visiting that Lady in the Woods. I knew no good would come of it, and now here we are."

"No good? This isn't about her. This is about me." Argo was facing his father with both arms crossed as well.

"No, this is about the tales she's been spreading in your head," he spouted. "Did she tell you to do this? Her stories aren't real Argo, they—"

"It's not your letter!" Argo held the letter up to his father. "It's not your letter! It's not your name on it!" His pent-up emotions came spilling out as he waved it between them. "If you want to sit here and wait for your time to come, then do it. That's your life, not mine. I choose to live mine by my decisions, and I will die by those decisions if I need to. You, my friends, this whole damn village can live like that, but the more I see it, the more I see that death isn't in those woods; it's here!" Something flowed and carried in his voice that was foreign yet natural. Passion bled in his words and filled the room. "Death has already taken the lot of you. The more I see it, the more I'm pushed to my decision. You all might as well do the same or take that sword off the wall and end it yourself."

His father was speechless. Emotion was flooding the home, and the fire raged even brighter than before.

Argo now stood with his hands on his waist, standing taller than his father had ever seen. His chest stuck out, and he looked like a grown man, his eyes burning with confidence though he was breathing heavily.

His father stared at the son he'd created. He conveyed his concern with his own fire in his eyes, one which burned a hole through Argo right down to his soul.

"I'm sorry Father... I need some time." He grabbed his cloak and ran out the front door. Wander ran after him and squeezed through the door before it could fully close.

CHAPTER 7

The Crew

Argo stormed down the quiet village road with Wander still following closely behind. Thoughts flowed heavily through his mind, and emotions only a man sentenced to death could understand. He found a tree stump near the village center where he sat and caught his breath. The decision of his remaining days was no light matter, and the choice he would make would, without a doubt, be the biggest one thus far. He was nervous and sad, but most of all defiant. Rage was flowing through him, which hadn't happened often in him or anyone else in his village.

He looked around from his lonely stump. A still tranquility rested around him. Wander sat and pressed herself against his legs, panting just as happily as she'd always done. He reached down and petted her behind her ear. It always seemed to have a way of grounding him. The bright moonlight cast shadows of the small, candlelit homes over him. This night, despite how unique it had been to Argo, was no different than any other for the people within.

Argo placed his head in his hands. He was pigeonholed, trapped in a corner like a rabbit he'd once enjoyed hunting. He could spend the last remaining days in the village, as he did every night, enjoying the company of his father and his friends. He could spend it with the Lady of the Woods, which was what his heart desired, but he knew deep down that the ending would be the same. No matter how he spent his time, he understood that his name had been called and his fate sealed. All roads led to the same destination. All except one.

The idea echoed in his mind, first as a faint call, almost a fly on the wall with his other ideas, then louder and louder, pushing its way to the forefront. He thought about how it would be to go into those forbidden Hallowed Woods and seek The Rider himself.

Did I just say that out of anger? Would The Rider be as kind to me as the others? Would he lop off my head with his giant broadsword? Can I even find him? His mind raced through the possibilities. *How am I going to act? Am I going to be brave? Or will I run and cower back to the village with my tail between my legs, only to be ridden down by The Rider?*

His blood rushed through his body as it had never done before. He could feel a pit in his stomach, and the hairs on his arms rose. He felt as if he were boxed in a small room and the walls were set to collapse in on him.

For him, these rare, unknown emotions felt the same as when he'd jumped down from his tree to face the danger of the boar. The thought grew louder and louder in his head, so much so that it now ran through his veins. His hands tightened into fists again and his gaze deepened.

He shot up from the log and confidently walked to Emeric's home, which lay only a stone's throw from the village center. He approached the dark and well-kept cabin, jumped the fence to the garden beside it, and went to the bedroom window, where Emeric's loud snoring could be heard from his bed.

Argo leaned in and called to his friend in a low voice.

The snoring stuttered, then Emeric turned over and pulled the covers higher.

Argo shook his head and told Wander to stay there. He leaped over the window and into his room, grabbed Emeric by the shoulder, and shook him awake.

This time Emeric awoke coughing, as if choking on his own breath. He squinted. "Argo?" he asked as he sat up and rubbed his eyes. "What are you doing here? Is this about the hunt? I said I was sorry."

"No," Argo replied in the same normal voice, now kneeling at the bedside. "It's something else. Meet me in the village center as soon as possible. I'm going to get Abaddon and Castor."

Emeric reluctantly agreed and shifted his feet over the side of his bed.

Once his friend started getting ready, Argo climbed back through the window and collected the others.

Castor and Abaddon also agreed with the plan, but they made sure to convey their annoyance. There had never been much to see in the village center, other than a bonfire burning throughout the night and beckoning those traveling to meet The Rider. At this point in time, all that was left of the great flames was a bed of smoldering embers.

The small path whose trail had run past the Lady in the Woods' house cut through the village square where they now assembled, illuminated only by moonlight and the dim glow of that once-ignited bonfire. The trail continued shortly past the village square and a couple of smaller homes. The trail finally jutted out like an ocean pier into a vast green ocean of grass, where it ended abruptly at the tree line of the forbidden Hallowed Woods.

The three tired friends trudged up grudgingly.

Wander greeted them as if all was normal. She hadn't the faintest idea about the reasons behind the odd meeting, yet she met them all the same.

Emeric rubbed his eyes again and yawned as he limped up slowly. A small blotch of stained blood soaked through the long strand of dark green fabric now tied around his wound. Castor, quiet and emotionless, looked as calm and collected as always. He hadn't piped a single word when Argo came to wake him. Instead, he looked at his friend and rolled immediately out of bed with no objections. Abaddon, tall and confident, looked strangely nervous as he approached. He alone of the group seemed to be the only one with the idea of the news that might follow.

Argo stood in the center of the trail, facing west, with the shadow of the flames dancing calmly on the cloak on his back. A cool wind blew softly through the group. "Well." He struggled to find the right words. Despite the many rehearsals in his head, he couldn't muster them at this moment. His hand nervously shot out with the letter.

And then there was no question. The group knew.

Emeric threw his hands to his head and turned around.

Abaddon grabbed the letter while Castor leaned closely to him, and together they turned to read it in the light of the fire. They showed it to Emeric, who squatted down and rested his hand on the ground. Abaddon put his hands on his hips and slowly shook his head. Castor stood with his arms folded and nodded in acknowledgment.

"Listen," Argo began. "Thanks for coming tonight. I'm sorry for the late night, but you all are my closest friends. And well…my fate is sealed. I suppose all of ours are." He put his hands in his pocket and looked at the fire. "I've thought about it. I could wait here until my days are up. But I'm not going to. Tomorrow I'm going to speak to the Lady in the Woods, gather my supplies, then go into the Woods and find The Rider myself."

A hail of disagreements went up, but Abaddon cut in over them.

"Argo, don't be foolish," he said. He wiped his hand over his face and put it back on his hips, shaking his head in disagreement. "You listen to too many of that Lady's tales. She filled your mind with delusion!" He must have realized how loud he got because he looked around and toned his voice into a yelling whisper. "Might have even cast a spell of some sort on you!"

The others agreed.

Argo didn't say a word. He let them continue.

"Argo, listen." Abaddon put his arm out toward Argo. "You can't go into those woods. First, it's forbidden. No one has ever gone into them, at least not in our time or to our knowledge. Second, you're dealing with tough news, and you're reacting in the moment. You need to take some time and gather your thoughts. Think rationally, Argo."

"Listen to Abaddon, Argo," Emeric cut in loudly. "We care about you. If it were one of us in your place, you'd be telling us the same."

Argo turned to Castor, who stared at the ground, sniffled, puffed his chin out, then nodded in agreement with the others.

"See! Even Castor disagrees with you!" Emeric pointed wildly at Castor.

Abaddon, standing in the middle of the two friends, stepped closer to Argo. "Look, you're brave. We all know it and acknowledge it. What more do you have to prove? Don't be foolish as well." He grabbed Argo firmly on the shoulders with both hands and almost smiled as he spoke. "We're blessed with a gift. We don't have to die and suffer like our ancestors once did. Don't waste it. It's not just for you; it's for us too. It's for your father. Your mother. The Lady. We don't wish to see you suffer. In there," he pointed down the path to the Hallowed Woods, "in there, there's only death."

Argo stayed silent. He made sure to take in every word from his friends. He knew this would be their reaction and had carefully prepared for it. He knew he sounded crazy and understood that his reaction now would drive how they would perceive his decision.

The young men continued to state their cases, and when they were done, a stiff, tense silence fell back on the group.

"I understand," Argo reassured them. "And you're right. All of you..." He paused and let his voice regain its confidence. "This is something I'm going to do. I know it doesn't seem logical, and I know that I have nothing to prove. I'm doing this for me." Argo heard the strength in his own voice, and it warmed him. "Look at us. We're all dying. We just don't say anything about it. Maybe I have heard too many tales. I know they're not real, but they're real to me. I can't go on living like this, and I know in my heart that I can't die like this. I want to use my last days to create a tale of my own." He turned and looked at the path going into the Woods.

"I don't know what's in there. Maybe it's nothing. Maybe it's just some old forest. Truth be told, I'm terrified of what I'm going to find, and of what's going to find me. I don't even like being out here in the dark. But I'm going, and that gives me more life than staying."

The boys protested loudly again, and Argo listened patiently.

Abaddon put his hand back on his shoulder and tried once again to dissuade him.

When it had finally died down, Argo continued. "I wouldn't ask any of you to join me, but if the same calling bellows in your heart as it does in mine, then come with me. I plan to depart two mornings from now at first light." With that, he turned and walked away.

***

The young men stood in place and watched their friend vanish into the night.

CHAPTER 8

The Consul

Argo lay awake restless that night. The thought of doing something that deliberately scared him also enticed him, lured him like a strange calling. "Argo the Brave" or "Argo the Courageous," he said to himself in low whispers as he lay sprawled across his bed. "Argo the Fool," he scoffed to himself, thinking back to the words of his father and friends.

After many hours, the first rays of sunlight broke through his bedroom window, by which time, he wasn't sure he'd slept at all. He hopped out of bed and got dressed as quickly as he could.

Wander lay asleep at the foot of the bed and opened one eye to watch her master race around the room. Her ears stood straight up, but she refused to move. Once she saw him open the door to the living room, she sprang up and followed him out the door.

Argo quickly gathered the few supplies he needed, tore off a piece of bread, and opened the front door, signaling for Wander to come with him. She ran toward him, then stopped just shy of the door. She turned around and ran back to her food bowl, grabbed whatever food she could stuff in her mouth, then cut back sharply and ran out the door and down the front steps.

Within moments, the two were on the path to the Woods of the East to see the Lady of the Woods. When they were two houses down, Argo checked his breast pocket for The Rider's letter and remembered that he'd left it on his bed stand. He turned around and ran back to his room, almost knocking the front door down in his haste. He opened the door to his room and paused.

The letter sat alone on his nightstand, still folded. He walked up to it and picked it up carefully. The moment sobered him, his hands feeling numb to the touch of the old paper that had been created solely for him. He felt the presence of The Rider with the letter. He carefully placed it in his breast pocket, immediately sensing it like the weight of a stone.

Wander placed her paw on him and broke him out of his trance, raising her paws as if it were a game she wanted to keep playing. He gently grabbed her, lowered her back to the ground, and gave her a strong and playful pet on her head. When he re-entered the living room, he stopped at his father's door. He could hear him snoring loudly in the room next to his. Moving quietly now, the two crept back out of the house and got back on the trail.

They moved faster than ever before and arrived at the Lady's home almost out of breath. The cabin looked especially radiant in the glow of the morning light. Dew rested and fell softly from the leaves in the garden, and the sounds of songbirds carried elegantly through the air.

Argo's heart beat loudly through his chest, and he felt as if the whole forest could hear it. He pushed past the gate and quickly walked up to the wooden door, where he knocked louder and more anxiously than ever before, despite trying his best to be gentle. Wander sat at his side, excited to be back at the Lady's home.

"One moment!" she called from inside. The hut had a strange way of appearing small from the outside, yet somehow manageably bigger when inside.

"It's me, Argo!"

Heavy bolts and latches turned from inside, and the door swung open. "Argo! I wasn't expecting you so early. What is it? What's wrong?" She looked just as put together as always, despite the early morning hour.

"I know. I'm sorry," he explained in between his heavy breaths. "I came here as soon as I could. I couldn't wait any longer." He extended his hand with the letter firmly grasped within it. The Lady recognized it immediately. Her shoulders dropped and she gave Argo a hug.

Argo didn't expect it. The warm embrace calmed him almost instantly, and he could feel his heartbeat slow and his breath normalize. He could feel tears swelling up in his eyes, so he pulled away from the hug to avoid starting a flood. Argo looked back to the path, wiped his eyes, sniffled, and followed the Lady inside.

The two went to the table, and the Lady sat down and examined the letter. She ran her thumb over the black wax seal, then broke it apart where it had been cracked and read the letter. Wander lay wearily at her feet, in a warm square of light made by the window. It lit her dark fur, and the hues of black and brown radiated beautifully. Argo stayed standing and leaned on the back of his chair for support.

ARGO

5 DAYS HENCE

The ink on the letter had somehow changed after midnight, to reflect an accurate count of the remaining days. The Lady laid it in the center of the table. She'd seen countless of these before from past travelers. "How are you feeling?" she asked.

"Well." Argo leaned heavily on the chair and moved his fingers across it. "I feel normal, I guess. I mean, a mix of emotions." He left it at that.

"Go on," she pried.

"Scared." He paused. "Excited. Nervous. I don't know. I don't know how to feel or what to expect." He gave the best answer he could.

"I see," she said in a reassuring tone. "So do all those who travel this path." She picked the letter back up and twirled it slowly in her hands.

"I thought I'd be ready for it, you know? We've all seen people come and go. It always seemed so easy. Especially for my mother." Argo thought back to the day she received it. "She was only given one day too."

"It's tough on everyone, Argo. Knowing our fate doesn't make it any easier to accept," she said. "Let me ask you something. Do you remember that flower we made tea from yesterday?"

"I do," he answered.

"Do you remember its colors? It's petals? How about the tea? Do you remember the taste?" she asked.

"I do."

"And your mother? Do you remember what she looked like? What her mannerisms were? How she acted when she first stepped out of her room in the early morning?"

He thought back to the early mornings in their home. "I do. I remember all of that about her. I don't believe I'll ever forget it. She was beautiful. Neat. Incredibly kind. She had a natural elegance to her. Even in the mornings she walked gracefully. Even when she got her letter, she was graceful in that too." Argo played with his hands on the back of the chair as he spoke. Realizing this, he let go and leaned his back against the wall, then folded his arms like his father had done.

"I was young then," he continued. "I didn't fully grasp the severity of it all at the time. I don't know, she seemed normal enough when it happened. I guess that made it easier on us, looking back. She made it seem like she knew what she was doing. Like it was easy. She had that way about her. A way of making us feel at ease. That everything was going to be all right."

The Lady let Argo's answer carry through the cabin until it came to rest peacefully among the silence. She stopped twirling the letter. "I see," she finally said. "Let me ask you something else, Argo. When we picked that flower yesterday, what could you tell me about the flowers surrounding it?"

Argo straightened up. "Well." He thought carefully but couldn't recall. He'd had too much on his mind to notice. "I can't remember."

"And your mother. When she came out of her room in the mornings, what did she wear? Did she have shoes on, or was she barefoot in the house?"

"Well, she... I think..." He fumbled over his words. "I really can't say." He felt almost ashamed that he'd forgotten.

"The reason I ask," the Lady continued, "is because I want you to understand what we remember. Beauty. Grace. Kindness. We remember how people and things make us feel. Old. Young. It doesn't matter, you see? What matters is what we do with the time that is given to us." She stood up from the table and filled a tea kettle with water.

Wander kicked awake with her movement, then quickly fell back to sleep.

"Now, the question I can feel between us is this: what are you going to do with the time that is given to you?"

Argo unfolded his arms and leaned back on the chair. The old wood creaked under his weight. "I came here because I need your help." He paused. "I'm going into the Hallowed Woods, and I'm going to find The Rider myself." He paused a minute to read her expression, though she remained stoic, so he continued. "I don't know anything about these woods, except for what I've heard in tales, mainly your tales. I don't know where to look or how to even find him, much less what to even do when I do find him."

The Lady hung the kettle on a little hook above the small fire burning in her oven. She let his words resonate in the air. "I see…" She adjusted the tea kettle and then rested again on the kitchen counter. "And when you find The Rider, what then?"

"Well, I expect to challenge him. That's the way I want to go out. I think that'll make the best story." Argo expected the Lady to laugh. In all the times he'd run through this conversation in his mind over the past night, he'd expected this to be the moment when the Lady would laugh and remind him that his plan was foolish. But she didn't. She didn't laugh, nor did she smile. She solemnly watched the fire softly lick the sides of the kettle. The heat emanated strongly from the fire and the flames grew bigger.

The absurdity of Argo's plans had not been lost on him. His friends and father had reasonable points. The easy path to his death lingered in the back of his mind. It would be simple and clean, and he could spend his last days enjoying his life. Since he'd made his decision to go into the Hallowed Woods and look for The Rider, he felt his soul walking a tight rope to stay on this path. The fear grasped his soul and pulled him off that rope and dropped him violently from that goal and into the comfort of that easy death. The terror and panic were just beneath the surface.

With every person he'd told and with every step toward that path, he felt the hole he was digging become so deep that looking to the surface revealed he might not be able to escape the way he had come. Yet another side of him wanted to keep on digging, the side that looked up from that hole and saw his friends, father, and the other villagers looking down at him. It made him angry. It made him defiant. They, in all their comfort and mediocrity, would stay the same in this life and into the next one. This was the only way they knew how to live. This cycle made him dig even deeper to escape the madness, dig to somewhere new. Anywhere. Just not here. And so he dug and would rather keep on digging than go back on his word and return home to cower for the rest of his days.

The Lady turned and looked into his eyes. Deeper than ever before. "That would be a fine story, Argo," she answered.

CHAPTER 9

The Vision

The Lady lit candles around the cabin and closed the windows. Small rays of sunlight bled in through the cracks of the blinds. The home filled with flickering candlelight and the dancing of the fire beneath the kettle.

"I've heard many tales, Argo, not all of which I've shared with you." She moved around the room, lighting more candles. "I've had many travelers pass by here on their way to meet The Rider, some visitors from lands far beyond your village." She lit the last candle and waved the flame. "You're not the first to venture into the Hallowed Woods, Argo. You are, however, to my knowledge, the first in a very long time."

Argo hung on every word. He pulled the chair back and sat in it.

"I have read about the Hallowed Woods before." The Lady sifted through books lined on her wall. She walked quickly into her room and continued her search. "The Woods hold many secrets!" she called from her bedroom, then came back out with a large book in her hands. The pages were dark, uneven, and bound by a leather cover that had green moss growing along the spine. She lay the book on the wooden table, and it landed with a hard thud.

"Listen, Argo. I have the tools to help you. But you must trust me." She grabbed a pail of water from beside the fireplace and set it on the table. Next, she calmly moved to her spice drawer, dug around, then shut it and sighed. She moved to her bookshelf and removed a couple of books from the top shelf, then pulled a small step stool toward her with her foot and stood on it, looking at the empty spot on the shelf. Behind the removed books, Argo saw that the bookshelf extended even deeper. She reached her hand in and pulled out a small wooden box that she added to the table before continuing to move methodically around the kitchen.

The teakettle screamed a high-pitched whistle. She wrapped her hand in a cloth and carefully removed the kettle from over the flame and poured some of it into a metal cup, then opened the small box and pulled out a handful of bright flower petals from it. Using a long set of tongs, she held the petals above the flame until they caught fire.

They burned with a bright blue flame that Argo had never seen before.

She let them burn for a moment, then waved the tongs to extinguish the flame and dropped them immediately into the cup, capping it with a lid. With her hand still wrapped, she slowly carried it to the table and set it next to the pail. "Now, when I tell you to, you're going to open that cup and inhale the smoke. Three breaths, you see?" She demonstrated for him. "Deep inhales."

Argo nodded. "Deep inhales. Got it."

After grabbing a set of metal tongs from the kitchen, the Lady reached them into the fire to dig out a burning orange coal, which she cautiously carried to the pail next to Argo.

"Now."

Argo removed the lid from the cup, closed his eyes, and inhaled the slowly rising smoke. It smelled of char and ash but carried a lively pulse he could feel travel through his nose and down into his lungs. The smell evolved to dirt and summer grass, then to a scent entirely new to him. Its vibrance and punctual warmth shocked his senses. He exhaled, and the smoke fell to the table and flowed off like water. Then he inhaled again.

The Lady watched, holding the hot coal over the bucket of water sitting in front of Argo. He exhaled and breathed in a third and final time, raised his head, and opened his eyes. His pupils swallowed the color in his eye. The candlelight flickered off their vast emptiness.

"Now, look into the pail," she commanded as she dropped the burning ember into the bucket. It plopped heavily and sprayed water over the table, sinking with a biting hiss. The water bubbled up violently around the coal.

Argo leaned forward and peered deeply into it. The water stirred and boiled, then died down into a calm darkness. He squinted and gazed even deeper. A connection from his eyes down to the root of his soul now intertwined with the water. Deep in the bottom of the pail, he saw a night sky filled with stars and swirls of magnificent dust clouds between them. There in the middle of it hung a bright full moon which cast its moonlight down over a beautiful spring meadow. High grass blew in the wind like waves on a lake.

Then he saw himself standing at the edge of the meadow, pulling at an invisible thread coming from his chest. Like the tales of sailors in a storm, he pulled with mighty heaves, reeling in an arm's length with every haul. *What lies at the end? What lifeline am I pulling closer with each and every pull?* The thread hadn't been tied around him; instead, it came from his chest, as if it were a part of him. Steadfast, he heaved and heaved, taking in wide armfuls in each pull, and with each one, the stars grew brighter and closer, as if he were pulling the sky down upon him. It drew nearer, then the thread pulled back on him so fiercely that he let it go. It raced from him furiously and then caught the end of its length. The force threw him face forward to the ground. Though he never hit it, he only passed through it and out the other side, as if in a new upside-down world.

He watched, then instinctively winced and looked away. He put his arms up to cover his face, though nothing happened. He still stood above the pail and peered back in and saw the moonlit meadow once again only as if seeing through tall trees with trunks thicker than any man. Two figures stood, swords drawn and facing one another. One, though shrouded in shadow, was undeniable.

The Rider. He stood straight as an arrow, with a large broadsword resting on his shoulder.

The other, a smaller figure, stood tall, proud, and unmoved by the menacing being across from him. His small sword paled in comparison to The Rider's, but he held it extended out in front of him.

The moon, twice its normal size, cast a shadow of the figures across the meadow of grass and wildflowers—wildflowers whose petals shined brightly with the same fluorescent blue light that the Lady had shown him in her garden.

The two now circled one another, swords drawn, then raised, then charging forward. They clashed together in the moonlight with a tremendous *crack*!

Argo flew back from the table, which he had unknowingly climbed and rested all his weight on, and thudded heavily against the ground.

"Argo!" the Lady said, rushing over with Wander. She lifted his head and looked at his face.

Wander wagged her tail wildly and licked his face. He lay on his back gasping, as if he'd just drowned. Beads of sweat poured down his face. He looked up at the Lady and wrapped his arm around Wander, pulling her away to stop her from licking. A bewildered expression with the weight of the sun fell across his face, as if he'd woken up from a thousand nights of rest.

CHAPTER 10

The Torch

Argo explained his vision as best as he could to the Lady, who listened intently to every detail. He spoke fast, and as he did, the hairs on his arms stood up and sent a chill through his body, which quivered down to his fingertips. He couldn't get the image out of his mind.

"No one can say what the visions mean," the Lady explained. "Much less if they're true or untrue, you see? All we can do is take them for what they are." She pulled back the chair and motioned for him to sit back down. "Now, I showed you that because I want you to see that there are forces at work greater than our understanding. I like to believe that this allows us to communicate with them in a unique way."

Argo sat down slowly, still perplexed by the vision. Wander rested her head on his knee and looked up at him. He put one hand on her head and scratched her behind her ear. He rested his head wearily in the other, unsure of what he'd witnessed.

The Lady took the seat across from him and let him have a moment of reflection.

"Wow." The gravity of his predicament fell upon him once again. The somber chill returned even colder than before, resonating through his bones. "I imagine this is how these things go. I don't want to assume that I am the swordsman, but to be honest, I want to be." He paused again, consumed by the experience.

The letter still lay in the middle of the wooden table. He reached and played with it in his hands. The Lady watched him silently.

The room fell quiet as he almost became lost in its words. "What more can man do against such a force?" he asked, perplexed. "We're all just struggling to stay afloat in this river, but to what end?"

"Well, it may not seem so, but we all have a choice, Argo. Never forget that; do you understand?" She leaned in closer. "Listen, I wish I could give you the answers you seek, but I can't, for I do not know them myself. Now…" She stood and walked to a chest in the corner of the room. "What I can do," she opened the chest and pulled out something long wrapped in an old linen cloth, "is give you this." She carefully wiped away the dust as she unwrapped a wooden torch inlaid with a band of rusted metal near the top filled with insignias engraved in a language he'd never seen.

He took the torch and studied it intently. It smelled of an old musk and mildew, as if it had been at the bottom of that chest for decades. The wood had been smoothed down over years of use.

"This was given to me by someone long ago." She opened her mouth to keep going but cut herself short. For a brief moment, she seemed almost choked up.

Argo noticed this and gave her a moment to continue, in which she promptly recomposed herself.

She explained, "The inscription at the top reads, 'Lead me from darkness into light'. I was told that this torch's flame blows toward death."

He looked down at the torch, his gaze returning to its crudely engraved text. "Thank you, Lady. This is more than I could've asked for" he said, despite not having the slightest idea of how helpful it would be.

"The last bit of advice I can offer you is this: Do not trust the Woods. Trust in yourself. Trust in your light above all else. That torch gifted to you is just a tool. Do not be so quick to trust its judgment. Death has no home yet lives in all things. Go with love in your heart. Do not be like the others. It is easy to be angry and resentful. True courage is to act with love in all things. You see?"

"I see," Argo answered.

The two hugged one final time. Then the Lady knelt and gave Wander a big hug as well. The dog licked her face, as she had always done. As simple as that, the two stepped out the door and down the path. The Lady stayed leaning in the doorway as they went, knowing full well that it had been their final meeting in this world.

The two headed down the path until they were almost out of view from the cabin. He stopped and gave one last look at her house, now with the door shut. The scent of garlic and wild herbs had faded into the filth of the forest. A tear welled in his eye and flowed down his cheek, and he gave Wander a firm pet on her head. He gripped his torch and slipped it between his belt and blouse.

The two swordsmen in the moonlight came to mind, then he headed home.

CHAPTER 11

The Night

Argo spent the rest of the day in the village square, livelier now than the night before. Villagers walked carelessly through it as they carried out their daily tasks. The usual smell of livestock and mud hung around. The air had become quiet and carried with it the faint sound of the goats and sheep that wandered constantly throughout the village.

Argo sat on one of the many benches that outlined the square, and Wander lay next to him, gnawing on a stick she'd picked up on their way back through the Woods. Villager after villager passed by aimlessly. Though the news that his name was next for The Rider spread quickly, no one showed any kind of sympathy for him, not even a glance or passing nod.

It was a cloudy and dull gray day. Each passing moment here was another assurance pushing him closer to his goal of heading into the Woods of the Abyss. The longer he watched, the more it pained him to think about living a long life here. The pain grew until he couldn't sit there any longer. "Let's go girl," he said to Wander as he stood up to walk home.

Through the open window of his kitchen, he saw the shadow of his father preparing dinner. The smell of a freshly-butchered goat—prepared with salted butter and herbs—floated out and over the road they walked. The rich scent filled the house like it had done years ago, when his father had made it for him and his mother.

Dinner passed uneventfully and without much conversation. Instead, a comfortable silence settled between him and his father.

After the meal, Argo's father sat by the fire and watched his son carefully lay out and wrap bread, preserved meat, and cheese, along with two waterskins—enough for a couple of days' sustainment if he rationed well—and a whetstone for sharpening his blades. Next, he laid out two flintstones which he could spark together with his knife to create fire and moved one to his knapsack, and the other where his knife, quiver, bow, and the Lady's torch lay together. Those he would carry on him in the event that he became separated from his pack.

His father carefully watched Argo's every move, sitting with one leg over the other in his chair near the hearth and puffing away at his tobacco pipe. He canted the chair so it was angled toward his son rather than the hearth.

Argo stood and counted the items he'd laid out. Then he carefully placed the bundle of wrapped supplies neatly in the knapsack and set it by the front door.

"I expect you'll take the dog," his father grumbled finally, nodding at Wander.

She lay sprawled across the floor next to her master and chewed vigorously at one of the great boar's hooves, her dark brown and black paws pinning it in front of her.

"I was hoping to leave her with you," he replied.

"This dog right here," he pointed to her, "you know as well as I that she won't leave you."

Argo gave her a look and tightened his lips. "I know. I can't though. Wouldn't be right. It's my time, not hers. Besides, what would I do with her?"

His father nodded his head in agreement, then took a large puff from his pipe and exhaled it slowly toward the hearth. "There's one more thing." He uncrossed his legs and stood, then carefully took the sword from above the fireplace. He held it out for Argo to grab. "Here," he said, holding it out to his son. "Who knows what you'll find there."

Argo traced the hilted sword in his father's hands. Never in his life had he seen this blade taken from the wall. "Are you sure?"

His father said nothing more but nudged the blade closer to him.

He grabbed the hilt and with some effort removed the blade. It was old, and small rust marks bled from the handle tightly gripped in his hands. Argo skimmed his thumb across the blade to assess the sharpness. It was as dull as the hilt it came in.

"It's going to need some care before you set out," his father said, watching his son hold the blade. They studied it together, then his father spoke again. "Son, listen to me." He placed his hand on Argo's shoulder. "I'm sorry for how our conversation went last night. Understand it was because I love you. Losing your mother and now my son is a cruel weight to bear for any man. I want you to know how proud I am to be your father and how proud I am to have raised you." His eyes shimmered in the light of the flames. "When your mother went with The Rider, I lay awake many nights wanting to follow her into those woods and bring her back myself. I never could. We wanted the best for you, and I wasn't going to leave you. Not that you need anyone to take care of you, but it's good to have someone there. I don't have the bravery that you do."

He sniffled and looked away, then composed himself and continued. "Alas, you are doing what I could not. You've made the choice to make this life uniquely your own, which as a father, is a fine gift to see. I don't know what you'll find in those woods or what fate awaits you. I know that there is no life for you in remaining here, and against my own wishes, I could never ask you to stay."

He patted his son on the back. "Go, my son, and show the same bravery to The Rider. Show him life." He pulled Argo in, and Argo sank into his father's arms and closed his eyes.

The two fell asleep in their chairs by the fire until at some hour of the night, Argo awoke and dragged himself to bed. Wander kicked awake and followed him. He lay awake on top of his covers, staring at the ceiling, not thinking of The Rider, nor the mysteries of the Hallowed Woods, nor even his friends or the Lady of the Woods. Argo lay awake, merely existing in the moment of time, thoughts drifting like a vessel on the sea, until the early hours of the morning, when he could see the first change of light through his window.

When dawn finally came, he rolled out of bed and had to lift Wander so he could tuck the sheets in as nicely as he'd always done. He carefully dressed himself in a clean set of clothes and folded his old set neatly in the corner.

His father was already awake and had prepared him some of the goat, cheese, and warm bread to eat before the journey. The two picked at their food and barely ate. They discussed Argo's plan of using the sun to head west, deeper into the Woods. Once he found The Rider, he was going to challenge him to the death. How that would play out, or if it would even come to that, was a mystery.

When they finished their meal, Argo slung his sword in its sheath over his shoulder and rested it across his back, then practiced reaching over his shoulder and drawing the blade. It was awkward at first, but after enough repetitions, he became comfortable with it. Next, he took the torch the Lady had given him and stored it at the top of his supplies inside the knapsack. He wanted to keep it out of the elements in case it rained heavily, as well as avoid losing it. Lastly, he threw on his knapsack, which rested comfortably over the sheath. His bow and quiver were strapped with thin leather straps to both sides of the pack. This had been the same setup he'd become accustomed to while hunting.

When he was fully equipped, the two of them stepped out the door with Wander following closely behind. Argo gave one last look at his house. It was dull, lifeless, and sat on a miserable plot of land. Yet for the first time in a long time, he saw a beautiful and humble home, despite its flaws. In his heart, he nodded a small nod of appreciation to the home, who, as Argo felt, nodded in appreciation back.

CHAPTER 12

The Departure

The sun broke through the tree line of the Hallowed Woods and slowly unveiled the dew-soaked grass along the trail. Argo, his father, and Wander passed through the village square, which was still empty of villagers. Not even the birds or livestock had awoken from their slumber. A small group of people was waiting at the end of the trail. Argo squinted and raised his hand to cover the sunrise from his eyes to see his friends, Abaddon, Emeric, and Castor standing empty-handed. Argo's father stopped him just shy of the group.

"Argo." His father stopped and turned towards his son, his thick hair barely hiding his sad and lonely eyes. "I'll say my goodbye here, and you can have time to make peace with your friends." He sniffled, then placed his hand once again on his son's shoulder and pulled him in for a hug.

Argo subtly nodded and pressed himself against his father for the last time in this life. He couldn't find the words to say goodbye, so he eventually said, "I'll do my best."

The two pulled back. His father's hand stayed on his shoulder. "If you find your mother, you tell her how much I missed her and how much we all still love her. All right, son?"

Argo nodded.

"And then you find The Rider." He pointed his finger in front of Argo's face. His heavy eyebrows furrowed, and his gaze deepened. "And you show him that the courage of men is not dead. Do you understand?"

He nodded again. "Yes, Father." The fear and anxiety that once gripped him had now been overcome with a sense of duty. Argo leaned down and looked Wander straight in the eyes. Her big brown eyes were a beauty to behold. "I love you, girl. You be good for Father." He wrapped his arms tightly around her. He couldn't hold his tears back. They poured out of his eyes like a violent stream. He placed his hand on her head and scratched behind her ears one last time. She let out a small whimper. The thought of leaving her tore away at him. He gave her a strong kiss on the forehead. Her fur smelled of dirt, yet it brought back all his memories with her. "Thanks for being my best friend, girl." He patted her head and looked up at his father, who then knelt on the ground and wrapped his arms around Wander to hold her tight. Argo placed his hand on his knife strapped on his belt, then turned and recomposed himself and walked confidently forward to his friends.

They'd been watching the exchange between him and his father, though they tried to appear as if they weren't. When Argo walked up, they stopped their conversation and looked at their friend silently. No greeting was needed.

"Are you doing well, Argo?" Emeric asked, then immediately turned around and coughed. He looked pale. His skin looked clammy and white, and he had dark circles around his eyes that were just beginning to become noticeable.

Argo clenched his lips and nodded. He looked down, then managed to say, "Yes."

"Listen," Abaddon said as he stepped toward him. "You shouldn't be doing this. It's a fool's quest."

Argo paused and gained the composure to utter what little words he had left. "So, I'm going alone?"

"Argo—"

"I understand," Argo said as he turned away to sniffle again. "You all have lives to live. You still have your time here. Can't say I wouldn't do the same." The pain of looking at his friends was too much for him. He looked up to keep the tears from falling. "I understand."

"Argo, you can't be mad at us because we don't want to join your suicide pact. That doesn't make us bad friends. It makes you a bad friend for demanding that of us," Abaddon explained.

"I'm not demanding anything," Argo said. He shrugged his shoulders. "You're right; I understand." The onset of fighting with his friends now sickened him.

"People are worried. There's concern about what this will do to the way of things," Abaddon said as he sidestepped to stand in front of Argo.

"What if going into those woods ends this for all of us?" Emeric quickly chimed in. "My mother said you're going to anger The Rider! What if you did kill him? What then—" He cut himself off and began coughing wildly.

Castor placed a hand on his back and tried to help him.

"Argo, listen to your friends," Abaddon continued. "People are afraid. They don't want you entering those woods. Think about them. Think about your father, and about our families. The villagers." His face tightened in frustration and began to turn red. "You're being selfish, Argo." His voice had become sharp with anger.

He let go of Argo's shoulder and took a couple of steps back. "Do you hear me? We should've stopped you from ever going to that Lady's house and listening to her tales of folly. They're myths, that's all. We live, we wait for our time, then we go with The Rider. That's how it goes. That's all it needs to be!" Abaddon walked away with those words, then immediately circled back. "You can't. You're not some story-tale hero, and this isn't some happy ending. This ends gruesomely. This ends with you dead in some twisted fate, and for what? Because you want people to tell your story? Well, they will, starting with me, about how I lost my best friend to madness because he tried to make something more of himself, and he did something he should've never done. The only story we'll tell is one of your foolishness. Maybe you should go, so no one will ever want to go again!" He looked away from his friend and walked outside the circle to cool down.

Argo nodded slowly, reflecting on every word. A tear rolled down his cheek and off his chin. He could still hear Wander whimpering with his father behind him. "So," he paused again, still nodding his head, "they think I can actually do it?" He looked at Abaddon directly in his eyes and lifted his shoulders back confidently. "So… they think it can be done?"

The group looked at him, and one by one, he looked right back.

He looked at Emeric. "And they're afraid?"

He gazed at Castor and took a step toward him. "Is this what we've become?"

He stepped toward Abaddon, who remained still. "Is this what the courage of men has led us to? A quiet life and an easy death?"

A sensation rose inside him, not of anger nor resentment, but of something natural. He stepped closer and the group took a small step back.

"Is this what we've become?" he demanded to know. "You listen to me, friends. This mediocrity. This fear. It's in our blood. This is who we are now. Look at that village." He pointed behind him. "Look at the passing bodies and faces. And look at you here, standing before me as messengers of the cowardly. We've become no better than the animals we hunt and eat. How many of us have come and gone without even a trace to our name? If my quest does end all of this, then so be it.

"Let the tales of courage and bravery return with me, even if only to break this trail of bleak misery of lives unlived. If it's a tale of foolishness and reckless ambition, then let it be as well. I refuse to wither away as so many have done before me. As you all are doing. Look at you. Infected as if you've taken an illness. You've let fear take root in your heart and seep into your bones. As deadly as any other disease."

Argo let the anger and disdain flow from his mouth. "If you're going to stop me, then draw your knives now and put an end to it. Stop me here and now. It may be the only good any of us do in our lives. Otherwise, step aside and let me begin." He looked each of them in the eyes, waiting for them to make a move.

He took no joy in speaking to his friends this way. He could feel the words cut with every breath and continued to let them do so. He felt like an animal, giving away to pure instinct when he spoke. The words of his dear friends beat against the integrity of his decision. They made him question his sanity.

Argo remembered his mother, who had walked as elegantly to The Rider as she'd done anything else. He thought of her love and her patience and how she would've reacted seeing him angry like this. He shamefully dropped his shoulders, humbling himself once again.

"This is not how I wanted to leave you," he said and paused briefly. "Forgive me." And with that, he pushed past the group that had once meant so much to him, and he marched to the end of the trail, through the grass, and out where a thin dirt path extended into the woods beyond.

He stopped and stood at the beginning of the tree line. The strong, sturdy limbs grew taller than any hut or cabin. They towered over him, and a cool breeze cut through the forest and softly caressed him as it passed by. It smelled cool and mysterious. The Woods were dark, and no songs of birds or wildlife came forth out of it, only the soft sound of the wind dancing among the leaves. His heart raced and his knees shook slightly beneath him.

He fought himself on whether to look back. Finally, he gave in and turned to see his friends still watching him, and then his father, whose arms were still wrapped around Wander to hold her still. Her tail was wagging anxiously, and she was fighting hard to break free. She barked once, then again, then was in a fury of barking, screaming at Argo's father to release her. Argo winced at the pain of seeing her cry. Beyond them, the trail continued to the gray and bleak village, which held no beauty nor sense of appreciation. Figures were now moving in and out of its streets, yet it seemed devoid of all life. It was cold and dull, and seeing it reinforced the sense of duty raging like a wildfire deep within him. He wanted to be mad, but that wasn't the right feeling for the time. His eyes swelled up once more.

He saw in his village the drowned potential of what it could have been. He saw the great deeds his people could have accomplished had they not diminished their light and sunk into the earth. It shook him because he knew that was now a part of him, perhaps the largest part of him, a weight that held him down beneath the surface. And now this heroic—more likely foolish—act symbolized him desperately clawing to stay afloat against that weight. Yet he was here, and the village was there.

He turned back to the trees, hiked his shoulders up to readjust his pack, and stepped forward into the forest. Wander's barking grew louder than he'd ever heard before, and in that sound was a cry almost unrecognizable. Something unworldly, as if her soul was grieving and spilling out from her voice.

Argo turned back instinctively in time to see her bite his father's hand and wrestle free of his grip. She broke like a bird in flight and sprinted toward the tree line, skirting beautifully at full speed through the group of young men and straight to her master, slamming against his legs. She held against them tightly.

He embraced her and looked up to see his father clutching the hand she'd bitten. He waved to Argo to say that it was okay.

Wander was going with him. Her will was set, and no force could break it. Argo, feeling relieved and loved, knelt and gave her a strong hug. He kissed her on the forehead yet again.

"All right. Let's go, girl."

Book Two

CHAPTER 13

The Woods

The Woods towered over them as if their tops touched the sky. Argo carefully placed each next step between webs of overgrown roots covered in bright green moss. Wander moved silently at his side. She understood the delicate nature of his movements and moved as he did, jumping from root to root and sniffing wildly at the earth.

A thin layer of haze rested all around and flowed softly through the trees like a stream. As Argo walked, the haze beat lightly against his face and glided smoothly around him, and though it was thick enough to be easily visible, he could still see a comfortable distance ahead. He wrapped his cloak around his body and held it in place with one hand. His other hand rested on the hilt of his knife strapped in its leather sheath on his belt. His nostrils swelled from the smell of a crisp, springtime breeze mixed with the scent of wet, soggy moss. Wander ran her snout over each root and base of each tree that they passed, which had trunks wide enough that Argo could hug one and not touch his own hands on the other side. He navigated between roots, fallen branches, and dry, crackling leaves of brown and tan. Between these, the dirt was soft and dark and sank lightly beneath him. Behind them, the open landscape of the village quickly became lost beyond the thick tree trunks.

After a few moments, the two were fully immersed within the grasp of the mysterious Woods. The trees reached tremendously high around him and rose straight up, as if they were arrows pinned to the earth. The sheer immensity of their height loomed over the two and made Argo feel smaller than ever before. The trunks stood completely bare of everything except for their bark, with branches stemming far out of reach, each one looking identical to the last. Looking up, he barely made out the rays of sunshine breaking through the canopy high above them.

The early morning light still shone from the east. *The sun's behind me, so I know that's east. If I keep that behind me, I'll be heading west, deeper into the Woods.* He thought of using the torch to help guide him, but he chose not to. Part of him was worried about where the flame would bellow, afraid of what it might reveal.

As they walked, the forest remained the same, as if they were passing through a moving painting that was repeating itself over and over again. Still, they pressed on with the light against their backs, moving ever so carefully in the maze of trees. Hours had gone by since Argo and Wander had first begun walking. He stopped beside a giant tree and took off his knapsack, looking around in all directions to get a bearing. It all looked the same, stretching endlessly and eventually fading into the hazy fog. He sighed and wiped the sweat off his face with his cloak. Then he dug through his pack and pulled out one of the waterskins and took a long swig, leaning his back against the tree. His legs felt weak, so he sank down until the point of his sword's sheath stuck into the ground. He awkwardly moved it out of the way and sat on the soft ground. Wander threw herself down next to him, panting lightly. He put the waterskin above her head and slowly poured a steady stream into her mouth. She lapped at it and drank until she had her fill and looked away. Careful not to spill any more, he put the skin back in his pack under the torch and sat there for a moment.

He looked around the scenery once again and realized that he had no idea where they were. Though worrisome, he was content since he also had no inclination of where he was going other than deeper into the forest. These thoughts drifted off as he rested, and eventually he thought of the letter The Rider had delivered. His heart beat fast again, and he rummaged through his pocket and pulled out the worn letter.

ARGO

4 DAYS HENCE

Another day gone. The weight of the writing sank into his gut. The hair on his arms stood up in goosebumps and his blood ran cold. He pulled his cloak snuggly over him. The words rang in his mind like a beckoning call, teetering on the verge of driving him to panic. He felt it rising in him, though he remained calm and acknowledged the feeling he was having. Part of him wanted to turn back and run back to the East, back to his village, and even to keep running past the Lady's home. He'd keep running as far as he could from these woods. When he reached the sea on the other side of the land, he'd get a ship and flee even farther, outside the reach of The Rider.

Why am I running toward *him? If I really want to make an impression, I should run* away *from him, all the way to the borders of the map. Make The Rider travel all that way just to retrieve a coward. I could make it so difficult to find me that maybe he'd give up and I could live my days peacefully.*

Argo wiped the sweat from his face again. *No. He would find me. I would live every day looking at the horizon, knowing that one day he would find me.* It wasn't Argo's way and he knew it. As much as fear and panic had struck his heart, he'd never allow himself to live so uneasily. He thought of his father and his mother, who both loved him so much. He thought of his friends, who were scared and wanted him to stay. He thought of the Lady, who brought him so much joy and wisdom and perspective on life. He knew that love was driving him forward, and despite the fear and desperation in his heart, that love would willfully continue to drive him to meet his fate head on, like the brave stories of old.

His thoughts raced to the Brave Hero Adonillis, who had gone through countless experiences like this. *Did he ever feel like this? Scared and afraid? Petrified with fear? Did he have a family? What drove him to live such a life? This would be so much easier if I could deflect arrows off my body or had the strength to lift boulders, just like Adonillis.* Argo flexed his muscles at the thought of it, but there wasn't much there.

Moments passed, and finally he determined he and Wander were well-rested enough to keep trekking. He accounted for all his gear and closed the knapsack, careful not to drop or leave anything behind. If this was a hero's journey, he didn't want to start with a foolish mistake.

The thin rays of light still beamed through the trees high above them. He looked warily up at the web of branches and leaves almost blotting out the sky, and he immediately felt uneasy at what he saw. The spears of light continued to come through the trees at the same angle as they had in the morning. It resembled the first light, but it had been hours since they'd left. *The light should be coming either straight down or leaning to the west. There's no way it's still morning.*

He sized up the forest. Not a sound outside of the ambient wind rustling the leaves. There were no birds or bugs, nor any of the other usual sounds he'd known forests to make, apart from the slight whistle of the breeze flowing through the trees. In one short moment, the forest felt strange and odd, as if the illusion that all was normal was broken.

This is too quiet.

Argo looked around desperately, but it all looked the same. The scene haunted him, and he could hear a high-pitched ring in his ears, which he had to have been imagining. He looked at Wander, who stood still and stared off in front of them through the fog as cluelessly as him, finding neither a trace of scent nor a sense of direction. *It's fine. I'll just continue keeping the sun behind me. Luckily, the wind is blowing from the same direction we've been walking. That has to be important.*

He pressed on, feeling more uneasy than ever before, but keeping the rays of light shining on their backs, but as he stepped, he slowly started to think he was walking by the same trees and same forest floor he'd already passed. He tried his best to push away the thought, but an uneasy sensation formed in the pit of his gut. His stomach dropped deeper and deeper with every passing step, his composure held up only by the thought of his father's words.

He gritted his teeth and pulled out his knife. It trembled in his hand as he held it out. He walked to the nearest tree and made a small horizontal nick with a slanted cut above to show the direction he was walking. Then he walked to the next tree and carved the same arrow in it, and so on in each tree as he passed.

Wander looked at him curiously. "This way we can have some idea of where we've been," he told her. Somehow talking to her out loud made him feel better.

They continued, carefully carving each passing tree. He didn't mind how slow the pace had become since he had no idea of how far they needed to travel. "How long has it been? Five? Six hours now?" he asked Wander. He peered behind his shoulder at the rays of sunlight still breaking through the canopy, still in the same position they'd been in all morning. On top of that, the fog, which usually disappeared after the early morning, was still the same as it had been, making it seem as if they hadn't moved a minute in time.

Argo thought back to the Lady's warning. *Do not trust the Woods.* The words replayed over and over again in his head. *Do not trust the Woods. Do not trust the Woods.* A light breeze flowed through the treetops, and the leaves danced gently against the light. Argo squinted and peered deeper through the beams breaking the canopy. He followed one of the beams against the light fog it reflected until it came to rest on a tree in front of him. Argo saw what it rested on and dropped his knife, which stuck point first in the dirt.

There he saw it. The pit in his stomach dropped into a lost abyss. He raised his hand and traced the shape of an arrow he'd nicked into a tree. It faced the direction he'd come from. His chest felt like it was being pressed in all directions. In every tree, a carved arrow pointed in a different direction.

CHAPTER 14

The Direction

Argo quickly picked up his knife without so much as looking down at it and ran his hand over the carved-out bark, then quickly drew it back. They were unmistakably his marks.

Wander ran around the tree and sniffed at its roots. She stopped and looked up at her master, who gazed desperately at the trees surrounding them. "No," he said under his breath in disbelief. "No…" His heart pounded wildly in his chest. Blood coursed through his veins faster than ever before, and he turned his head in all directions, looking for an answer. "How? How did this happen?" he asked out loud in a low voice that cut through the thin silence of the forest. He leaned over and rested his hand against the rough bark.

He wrestled his pack off and dropped it to the ground, then squatted and pressed his back once again against a tall tree. As before, his sword stuck in first, and instead of moving it, he rolled to the side and let it stick up. Tears welled, and he fought back the urge to let them fall.

Wander approached and licked his face, then wagged her tail and sat down beside him before letting out a wide yawn and then a long sigh. She lay down, resting her head on a root. Argo kept his eyes focused on a leaf on the ground beside him and wrapped an arm around her. "I'm such a fool. I should've listened to them," he said, thinking back to his friends that morning. He looked at Wander, who was now fast asleep, and he ran his fingers through her dark fur. Now the restrained rush of tears rolled down his cheeks.

"Do not trust the Woods. I might have messed up bringing us here, girl," he whispered slowly, resting his forehead in his palms. "Now we're victims of this cruel game. We could've just stayed home and lived out our days peacefully with friends and family and a warm bed."

Wander awoke and rested her head on top of his knee.

"This is it. This is the tale of Brave Argo," he told her. "Argo, who so boldly killed himself and his dog. Who would tell this tale except mothers to their children as a lesson of blind ambition?" The idea of a quiet life and gentle passing had never seemed as appealing as it did now. The weight of his situation fell heavily on his shoulders. Now they were no more than animals stuck in a trap. The same fear he'd once laid on the beasts he hunted now came down upon him. He saw life coming full circle as he, the hunter, had become prey to a force he didn't understand, yet he could feel its gaze upon him, slowly and surely bleeding the life and hope he cherished.

He rummaged through his knapsack and brought out the torch and his flintstone, then set the torch down and struck his knife violently against the flint. Sparks danced from his blade and into the pocket of the torch. After several hopeless strikes, the embers stuck. Argo cupped his hands around the pocket and blew gently. The ember grew into a small, flickering flame, like a chick carefully hatching from an egg. He picked the torch up by the handle, and the modest flame grew high. It swirled in a circle, as if the wind was blowing in all directions, then blew toward Argo, as if the wind had chosen to blow it there too. He moved the torch to his side, and, as if to confirm his suspicion, the flame stayed blowing toward him.

This can't be good.

Wander watched his every move carefully. He waved it to the other side, and again the flame stayed pointing in his direction. He threw the torch down, and it landed with a heavy thud on a bed of leaves. The flames quickly spread, so he immediately sprang toward them and stomped them out. He grabbed the torch off the ground and dug out a small area of dirt with his foot, then put the torch out against it.

His breath sounded stiff, and he could hear his racing heartbeat in his ears. The flame had shown him what was true, and what he should've realized from the start—he was a doomed man, and doomed men who know their fate are no different than animals backed into corners or caught in a snare. They're all the same, and the knowledge of this etched itself into Argo as surely as he'd etched his own mark into the tree—the marks that had betrayed his direction and led him to this peril. Argo had seen this before in his hunts and often on sleepless nights, he'd wondered what he'd do if it were him being hunted and not the other way around.

"The only option is to fight back," he said to Wander. "If the animal doesn't fight, it makes it easier on the hunter. If he does fight, no matter the odds, he gives himself the opportunity to escape, and at the very least, makes it more difficult for the hunter." The act of speaking out loud helped him feel less alone. Wander paid no attention to his words and instead rested her head on the forest floor.

Smoke rose from the blown-out torch in his hands, and he was now lost in his thoughts. He reached over his shoulder and drew his sword from its sheath across his back, holding it confidently in his hand. The worn leather on the handle fit neatly into his palm. He gripped it as he had done several times in his dreams, and while pretending as a child. The light reflected off its blade in his eyes. He turned it away and saw a crude reflection of himself in it. His face was flushed red with emotion, and he looked weak, shameful. He waved the blade away and looked again at the torch, then his pack next to it, and once again back up to the beams of light pouring down from the trees.

I am now the animal.

Wander was sleeping peacefully on the ground, stirring his admiration for her trust in him and how she followed him in here without question. He felt in his soul a deep obligation to see this through. His fingers clenched tightly around the leather grip of his sword. He turned the blade to see himself in its reflection.

CHAPTER 15

The Choice

Argo repacked his knapsack and lit his torch again. It didn't matter if the flame bellowed back at him, he was going to trust his intuition and keep moving forward. When the embers caught, the flame whipped wildly in circles, then stopped and held vertically. He gave the flame time to settle and gain its bearing, and it calmed, then licked in the same direction from which the rays of light shone. A hopeful feeling returned to him when he saw them still pointing forward.

While he was initially resistant to trusting the flame, it now blew in the same direction he'd decided to go. The gentle breeze flowing through the trees now cut through Argo and his torch, yet the flame remained steadfast against the wind. With the torch firmly held in his left hand, and his sword confidently in his right, he picked up speed and continued his quest in the labyrinth of trees. Wander became more alert too and trotted beside him.

Argo walked with newfound confidence. He wore the same look on his face as when he'd first stubbornly entered the Hallowed Woods against his friends' wishes. He still, as he had then, didn't care where he was going. *If fate already has me in its clutches, then go ahead and take me. If I wanted to die in place, I would've stayed in the village.*

Within minutes, he spotted what appeared to be a clearing in the forest ahead. The thin layer of fog cleared out enough for him to make out an opening in the canopy. The sun beamed through the trees brighter than before. He quickened his pace as he navigated his way over the large mesh of roots. The opening appeared larger and larger, and his pace became quicker and quicker, until suddenly he understood what the opening was.

Argo paused in disbelief. The flame billowed toward the clearing, then up the abruptly finished path and straight toward his village. *How? The sun stayed behind me all day. I had to have been heading west. Unless the forest played some kind of game with me, it should be impossible to be back here.*

Behind him, the sun finally began to set. Brilliant hues of orange and red painted the sky. Only moments ago, he was wishing he was back here, and now that he was, he didn't feel as at home as he would have expected. He didn't feel comforted, nor excited, nor even happy at the sight. Instead, an overwhelming grief of failure swept over him.

He pictured himself walking through the village square and people asking him what had happened, only for him to explain that he'd failed and gotten lost and scared, and that he was just a foolish boy who'd acted out his half-witted dreams. The idea of being one of them was now terrifying to him, despite how appealing the idea seemed when he broke down moments earlier. He saw it now in its true light. Despite everything he thought before, going back would be cowardly, and that stung Argo deeper than anything. He understood more than anybody in that village that some wounds never leave a man.

He quickly extinguished his torch and remained far enough inside the Woods to avoid being detected. Wander made no attempt at leaving him or running off into the village. After this morning, she would be reluctant to leave his side again. Far off in the distance, he saw the daily bonfire rise in the village square, which took place every night at sundown. The smell of burning wood blew toward him and washed a sense of comfort over him, like a lullaby calling him home. *A bonfire would be amazing right now. A warm hearth and good tobacco are all I really need.*

Argo realized the trance he was falling into and shook himself out of it. He sat behind a tree and stared at the village while he formulated his plan. He decided it would be better to move farther into the Hallowed Woods and set up camp for the night, far enough out of view to hide the light from his own fire, but close enough to not lose the opening. He stood—and noticed a group of villagers gathering in the village square. Outside of certain holidays, he couldn't remember the last time anything like this had happened. The group had met too far out of view to make out any details, but he saw many of them holding torches. They all faced his direction.

"They must be talking about us," he whispered to Wander. Disappointment swept over him. He hated the feeling of hurting anyone or doing anything to upset people, and now he felt it more than ever. The torches bounced up and down in the crowd as if in anger. Loud cries and shouts echoed through the cloudless night, though he couldn't make out any of it. *If they're talking about me, they must be bringing my father and friends into it. I hope they're not blaming them.*

"If we go back, who knows what they'll do to us. But do you think they might be hurting Father?" he asked Wander. "Or our friends? We're already here, and this is so much more than us. You saw how they reacted when I came in here." He paused and watched the mob bicker at each other. "I can't. My soul is telling me to keep on the journey, and my mind is telling me to go back. But I have to stay true, girl. Remember what The Lady and Father said." He placed his hand on Wander's head and scratched her behind her ears. "Let's get out of here before we think too much about it and run out of daylight."

He grabbed his gear and walked deeper into the Woods, taking one last look at the village, the roaring bonfire, and the growing crowd behind him.

CHAPTER 16

The Night

The night swept quickly over the Woods. Argo found a flat area between the trees and set up a small fire far enough away to not allow the light to be seen by the villagers. The cool breeze remained steady and provided him some comfort as it passed by. The fire, though small and unimpressive, gave enough heat to warm him and Wander, as well as enough light to see comfortably.

His stomach growled once he smelled the burning campfire. Wander must have felt the same since she was staring at him and had a bead of drool hanging from her mouth. He dug through his knapsack and pulled out the preserved meat, bread, and cheese, then carefully cut small slices of each with his waistband knife. He layered the slices and nibbled at them as he stacked them one on another. Between bites, he made one for Wander, who promptly ate the entire stack in two bites. She finished it and sat next to him, staring at him for more. He ignored her. She put her paw on his forearm. Her nails were sharp and dug into his sleeve. He grabbed her paw with the other hand and set it down. "That's it, girl. That's all we can have tonight." She stared at him and cocked her head to the side, then she understood the message well enough. She let out a sigh and coiled tightly in a ball against his side, resting her head on her tail and leaving her ears comfortably lowered.

Argo pulled her in tighter and covered part of her with his cloak, then continued eating his dinner in small bites to make it last. As all men do in the presence of fire, he peered deeply into the flames, as if they were speaking to him.

The untethered flames let his thoughts run wild. The air remained still and quiet, and only the sounds of crackling sticks filled the air. The smell of the burning campfire reminded him of all the nights he'd spent at home by the hearth. Now the smell was weaker and mixed with the cool forest air. Though it was different, the sense of homeyness was still there.

Argo had never camped out before. As far as he knew, the village allowed it, but no one ever did. He'd heard about it several times in stories of The Great Hero Adonillis, but that was it. However, he had often prepared for a hunt by trekking through the Woods of the East before sunrise or, if a hunt carried on too long, into the night. But even then, his friends had always accompanied him.

The mystery and elusiveness of the Woods escaped him now. He felt almost at a strange peace in a strange land as he sat next to the fire and watched its flames and felt its warmth. The world drifted away, and all that remained was here, lit by the firelight. Thoughts of his journey hadn't quite left his mind, but presently, he felt captivated by the moment. He felt like an actor, playing the part of some great adventurer or hero, almost to the point where he felt like an impostor. His sword lay closely by his side, and he had his knapsack close behind him to lean on for support. He moved his hand and held the hilt of his sword, not for the purpose of defense, but just to reassure himself that it was real and that he was actually on a quest.

While most would feel cautious from the idea of sitting alone, except for Wander, next to a fire in foreign woods, Argo felt no such feeling. He felt more at peace in this moment than he had lying in his own bed. Perhaps his pride was keeping him so peaceful since he was doing what he'd said he'd do. The drive of creating his own story lit a fire in his soul. He thought of the villagers, comfortable in their cozy beds and warm homes, and he felt a sense of pride to be out in a foreign land. The night carried on, and Argo let his mind detach like a ship without a port. Each thought drifted peacefully to the next. His eyes felt heavy and started to close on their own.

Snap!

The sound of a stick being broken came from a jet-black area of darkness between the trees in the distance. He immediately turned in its direction, and Wander stood up. Her ears were fully perked, and a low, rumbling growl came from deep inside her. The fur along her spine stood straight.

Argo gripped the hilt of his sword and stared into the blackness. Light from the campfire reflected off two eyes in the darkness. His eyes met with them for a split second. They blinked and were gone, leaving only obscurity. He stood and held his sword out. The hair on the back of his neck stood up, and his heart raced so loudly that he could hear it, yet he remained calm on the outside. Wander stayed focused on its direction, her growl, terrifying.

Whatever it is, it can see me, but I can't see it. He scanned in all directions, but only the black curtain of night was with him. Silence fell over the forest once again, and all became still.

Wander dropped her guard and relaxed as best as she could. Argo circled the campfire and stared off into the darkness around them. Whatever was watching him had now fled. Weariness crept over him again. He sat with his back against one of the large trees near the fire and lay his sword across his lap. He quietly called Wander over to sit next to him, and she listened.

The rest of the night remained quiet, and Argo spent most of it staring into the campfire, wondering what creature had been watching him. Now he felt uneasy and even more like an animal being preyed upon. He kept his hand gripped tightly around the hilt of his sword until fatigue overtook him and he drifted off into a deep, powerful sleep.

He awoke huddled over on his side and curled into a ball underneath his cloak. Wander remained rolled up tightly next to him and seemed as comfortable as ever before. The morning sunlight broke through the canopy and rested easily on Argo's eyes. He stirred and shielded them with his hand. Steady smoke rose from the embers of the once-burning fire and dissipated seamlessly into the air. The smell of charred ash and smokey timbers stoked his appetite.

The forest now teemed with life. Birds and crickets chirped and sang their songs, which carried through the air as beautifully as the morning light. These were all familiar to Argo, having been hunting so many times before in the early morning hours. He propped himself up and wrapped his arms around his knees. The morning air was fresh and smelled of a warm spring morning. He rummaged through his pocket and pulled out The Rider's letter.

ARGO

3 DAYS HENCE

The days were slowly withering away, one by one. At times, it was hard for him to comprehend his position, and at other times, he understood it entirely. Being forced to deal with such life-altering scenarios outside his control had been a difficult concept to grasp. He couldn't say how he felt now. A potent mixture of impending doom, fear, and uncertainty contrasted with a rising concentration of duty and pride in the quest he was undertaking. *Did my mother feel like this? Or the others who'd gone so easily with The Rider?*

His thoughts turned to The Rider and how little he knew about this man. Even while on horseback, he stood taller than any man Argo had ever met. His hooded cloak hid his figure, yet the strength and poise underneath were plain to see. The Rider's armor-clad gloves tightly gripped the reins of his mare, whose chainmail and plated armor thudded together with every heavy step. He remembered that when the villagers saw The Rider, they never felt fear, perhaps because they strangely felt that The Rider was somehow on their side. The unspoken pact he'd made with the travelers provided the only solace between them.

Argo dug through his pack and pulled out the bread, meat, and cheese again. He took some for himself and broke off an equal part for Wander. She inhaled the food as quickly as she could and sat staring at him.

"No," he said. "We have to make it last." He gave her a playful pet on her head and kissed her on her forehead, forgetting the terrifying thoughts about The Rider. "I'm glad you came with me, girl." He smiled at her. "Let's pack it up and get moving." Argo stood and carved a large "X" in each direction of the tree he'd camped in front of. If he was to get turned around like yesterday, he'd have a landmark to recognize his campsite. When finished, he sheathed his knife and stood there, contemplating the marks he'd made. He pulled out his knife again, and under each "X," he scratched a number "1." The way he saw it, he was going to be spending multiple nights in the Woods. It might be best to at least label the campsite with the corresponding night he slept there.

Satisfied with his markings, Argo packed away his belongings and relit the torch. The flames wisped and twirled in the nimble breeze, then came to settle in a small and comfortable flicker, which pointed in the same direction as Argo's village.

"Well, this torch doesn't instill much confidence," he said almost half-jokingly to Wander. "So, we know the village is that way, which is where the flame is pointing, so I think we should go the opposite direction, deeper in the forest…" He paused to think about his logic. "I feel that our fate will meet us where it's already decided to meet us. All we can do is try to find our way. It's drawing us closer and closer with each passing day. I can feel it. We are like ships without a port, destined to tides of the sea."

He stood in the silence of the forest, feeling the gravity of helplessness he was in. The trees seemed to tower taller than they ever had before, and a feeling of powerless dread swept over him. Wander offered his eternal smiles and pants. Argo knelt and gave her another scratch behind her ears. She was in an ignorant bliss, which Argo couldn't help but admire.

CHAPTER 17

The Ruins

The two set off away from the village, once again turning their backs to the only life they knew. Argo felt somehow different about this leg of the journey. The Woods were now alive with wildlife, their songs drifting through the air, which gave him a small sense of comfort and assurance that this day would be different from the cold and lifeless one before.

As they walked, the scenery and terrain slowly changed as befitted a natural forest. The trees dug deep into the earth, and they rose and fell with the slight hills rolling through the woodland. The fog had cleared, and the woods beamed with a new life. Wander trotted along happily next to him, navigating over roots and between the tall, sturdy trees. Dark green moss covered the bases of the trees and grew along their massive trunks to knee and chest height.

Argo started the day by continuing his method of knocking arrows in every tree. This slowly faded to every other tree, and then he stopped almost entirely as he felt comfortable navigating. The sun was rising behind him, and the bright rays shifted as the day progressed.

Sometime in midmorning, the two heard running water. Wander trotted over happily and lapped at the small stream. Her tail was wagging and only stopped momentarily as she drank. While she refreshed herself, Argo knelt over the flowing water and traced its path through the Woods. The water was as deep as his longest knuckle and flowed clear and beautiful.

He assumed the water ran northeast, since he and Wander were traveling west according to the morning sun, but as he'd learned the previous day, even that was not to be trusted. He reached into it and filled his hand with the water, then used it to wipe away the sweat and dirt from his face. Off in the distance and through the trees, he noticed a stone wall downstream. He rinsed himself once more and topped off his waterskin. He met eyes with Wander and motioned with his hands for them to keep moving. She caught on and took one last lap of water, then jumped to follow her master.

Suddenly, a structure revealed itself through the tall trees—not just one but several ancient houses built of stone and standing in a circle. The small village had long been swallowed by the grips of time, and what had once been sturdy homes now lay in overgrown ruins. Vines and moss hugged dearly to the walls, and most of the roofs had caved in. The gray stones lay scattered across the ground, lost in the mess of moss and grass which reeked of decay and mildew.

The two followed a small stream flowing behind one of the houses and they continued on its path through the trees. Argo and Wander walked with curiosity to the nearest home and peered into the empty space in the wall where a window had once been. Wander got up on her hind legs and placed her paws on the stone. Nothing but crumbled ruins and overgrown foliage lay inside.

They walked around the small house, and in a space above the front door, Argo made out a light inscription through the vines. He reached up and cut some of the foliage away to read it. It looked as if someone had painstakingly carved a message into the stone. Though faded over time, each letter laid deep and clean cut. The writing was in a language he didn't understand. He stared at it as if its meaning would somehow dawn on him. Wander looked curiously at him. He turned to her and shrugged. He turned his knapsack around and pulled out the torch. Some of the letters were the same. It had to be the same language. He tucked it neatly back into his pack.

The two walked curiously through the first home and found nothing but crumbled stones mixed in a bed of weeds and moss. Not even Wander's keen sense of smell could pick up a trace of any unusual scent. Nothing and no one had been there in ages. The sunlight that broke through the hole in the roof lit up the once-humble home and came to rest gently on the green and gray floor. Argo looked through the hole and then at the rest of the roof, which seemed to be precariously held in place by no more than a few stones waiting to fall.

As they exited the house, Wander froze. Her nose wiggled and her tail shot straight out. She'd picked up on a scent. She put her nose close to the ground and swept all around them. Her pace quickened. She went up to the second house and traced the outline of the outside wall with her snout, following it around the corner.

Now Argo was hot on her trail as they approached a third stone house that had been heavily damaged. Wander sniffed around the low corners of the outside wall, and then stood on her hind legs once again to look through the opening of what had once been a window. Argo crept up next to her, looked through the ledge, and immediately crouched behind it. He pulled her down and held her firmly at the top of her neck.

He cautiously looked over again. He heard the low grumbling of a colossal wild boar, though something seemed strange about him. The massive beast stood feasting on a bed of mushrooms just beyond the stone village and was facing away from them. Argo slowly peeked his eyes over the window ledge and took in every bit of his immense being. He looked bigger than the boar he and his friends had taken down just days prior, standing almost at Argo's height, even on all four legs. His putrid odor of sweat and fermented wet fur hit Argo immediately and he almost choked. The creature grunted loudly, then turned in their direction. Instead of massive tusks, he had fully grown antlers stemming from the sides of his mouth, reaching high above his head. Each one branched into a sharp spike that glinted in the sunlight.

Argo ducked behind the wall before the creature could see him, and he quietly drew his sword from its sheath. It got caught on something and stuck to itself, pulling the whole sheath upward. It hit against the wall but luckily didn't make a sound.

Wander's hair stood straight up along her spine. Her lip was gnarled and showing her white sharp teeth. She remained quiet as ever and watched her master carefully, yet was ready to strike at any moment.

Argo cautiously moved the sheath aside and drew the blade out fully, holding it close to his chest. He shut his eyes and tried to slow his breathing, and glanced at Wander, who was still watching from behind the wall. He gently tapped on his leg to get her attention. She turned to him, and he put his finger over his lips and pointed the way they'd come.

We need to get out of here. Now.

He was sitting with his back against the wall, his heart beating heavy in his chest. His stomach retched with fear, and he struggled to control his breathing. A flash of light shot across his eyes and caused him to jump, though it was only sunlight reflecting off his polished sword. He turned it again and saw his own reflection and an unfamiliar look of fear staring back at him. He tightened his hands around the hilt and looked across the opening at the second house, then gave a look at Wander. The beast grunted loudly again and gnawed away at the mushrooms.

Staying low, Argo slowly crawled on his hands and knees to the second home, still holding Wander close by her neck with one hand while carrying his sword in the other. The second house had seemed so close before, but now it seemed a world away. At half the distance to the second house, Wander still in his grip, he heard a sudden, tremendous crunch from his foot stepping through a dead log hidden in the grass. All sounds from the monster stopped, and all was now quiet, as if the entire forest waited.

Argo stood still, frozen in time.

Thud.

The beast took a step forward. The ground shook when it struck.

Thud.

A heavy crunch of something crumbled beneath his second step.

Thud.

Argo and Wander stood as still as the structures. His blood rushed and he fought all instincts to flee. Wander remained steadfast with her master. She crouched and kept her head and tail low to the ground, baring her teeth aggressively though making no noise at all.

Thud.

Behind the corner of the wall, the immense antlers of the mammoth beast were now in view. Their points were sharp as any arrowhead. He steadily walked out from behind the wall and turned his head to the left and then to the right. His dark-black snout sniffed and grimaced as it swept where they had just been.

The two remained remarkably still, watching in horror as the beast took another step forward, revealing his giant, meaty head.

Thud.

His torso was now fully out of the doorway. He turned and his eyes locked with Argo's. The beast reared his head back and gave a thunderous cry.

"Go!" Argo yelled to Wander. "Go go go!"

The two bolted to the second house. Argo leaped through the window and tumbled heavily on the other side, sword still in his hand. Wander ran around the side.

The boar roared again, then reared back and charged, galloping with heavy booming thuds in their direction. Argo ran through the ruins and threw himself through the far window. The boar slammed into the rock wall behind him. The wall crumbled. The structure collapsed. Stones spilled.

Wander ran around and found Argo. She barked and growled ferociously. Argo had tumbled again after his landing but had struggled to his feet, and now he sprinted desperately back to the first house.

The boar roared and whipped his head from side to side behind them. The brute had exited through the broken doorway and madly shook his head again, unphased by the pain. He spotted Argo and stomped his feet wildly against the stone rubble.

Argo and Wander ran even faster to the first structure. Wander jumped through the window. Argo, close behind her, vaulted over the same window ledge and landed on his feet. He ran through the collapsed house and flung himself through the far-side window again. His pack swayed and shook as he moved through the stone hut. He made it through the window and stopped on the outside to grab Wander by the back of the neck and pull her up and through.

The beast charged madly and hit the far wall. An explosion of debris scattered across the forest.

Argo watched through the window as the beast stood inside the home, momentarily stunned by the force of the wall. Suddenly, a loud *crack* ripped through the air as the roof collapsed on him. The stones gave way with such force that the creature's legs gave out under him and the beast collapsed under the weight.

"Let's go, girl!" Argo grabbed her, and the two ran to the far side of the circle and into another structure taller than the rest. Despite a collapsed roof, it was still the most well-preserved of the homes. They ran through the doorway and looked around desperately. Gray stones and bright green grass covered the floor, which was littered with piles of fallen debris.

Wander ran to the far corner, where a set of broken stairs led up to a second floor that had crumbled and fallen into ruins on the lower level. A small platform of the floor supported by a wall below it, remained at the top of the stairs. They hurried across the ruins and up the stairs. Argo quickly set his sword to the side, took off his pack, and rummaged through it. But through a large part of the missing wall, he saw the collapsed stones of the first house stirring from the angry boar. The beast hidden beneath was still alive and struggling violently to break free. Fumbling wildly, Argo threw off his pack and pulled out his flint stone and the torch. Then he got his knife and struck forcefully at the stone. Sparks flew everywhere, and those that made it to the torch immediately died there. He struck at the stone again, his fingers moving faster than his thoughts. Nothing. He tried to strike again, and the stone flew from his hands and bounced on the floor. It stopped, hanging over the edge of the wall. He dove and caught it before it could fall, his hands shaking uncontrollably.

"All right, all right. Careful. Slow down," he muttered.

Wander climbed down a couple of steps and barked viciously at the first house. Argo didn't look up. He struck the stone once more, and this time the sparks stuck and created a small ember in the pit of the torch. He threw the stone by his pack and slid his knife back in the sheath. He'd done it so many times that the motion was smooth and fluid. He cupped his hands around the ember and blew slowly on it. Wander barked and growled with everything she had. She burned for a fight.

Argo continued to blow gently on the glowing ember until it caught and took on a small flame. He finally looked back at the first house and saw the beast had freed his head and was now shaking viciously to free the rest of his body. His massive antlers were swinging from side to side to rake off the stones. Argo gripped his sword tightly in his right hand. The longer he waited, the harder it would be to act. He had to strike now, and fast—before the fear truly set in. With the torch held firmly in his left hand, he cautiously encroached on the beast.

The pile of stones rumbled on top of his foe's body. Argo stood in front of him as he struggled to escape. Argo held the torch nervously between them, the flame of his torch rising and roaring wildly, pulling itself closer as if on its own and desperately trying to lick the beast's face. Argo raised his sword high in the air, intending to deliver a killing blow, but froze. He looked into the beast's eyes and instantly became entranced by what he saw. The boar let out a piercing cry of agony and looked fearfully at the fire held in Argo's hand.

The beast's eyes told Argo everything in the world. He saw fear, fear which Argo knew himself, deep in the furthest recesses of his soul, the same helpless fear he felt and saw in his own reflection—an insatiable agony and terror of his impending finality. In an unmistakable moment, Argo felt more than a deep connection to this animal. They were one and the same. He'd been relentlessly haunted by the fear he now saw in the boar's eyes, which were so simple, dark, and black, yet they held the world together. They were portals, and in that moment in time, Argo felt his soul peer into the window of this animal's being.

Argo felt the torch and the sword in his hands and was disgusted with where he stood. He understood the life and death challenge they were entangled in, and he almost hated himself for being the victor. He could've easily taken the torch and burned the animal as it lay in the trap, and the animal knew this. But Argo couldn't. The Rider could easily do the same to Argo. He was in The Rider's snare the same as this boar was in his. The sword and the torch gave him power. He saw the thin veil that lay between life and death and understood what an easy flick of the wrist could do to drastically alter the life of this being, be it a man or beast. Argo felt shameful. He felt powerful, and he felt hurt.

Wander barked furiously, and Argo was ripped from his trance, still standing with the weapons in his hand. He looked at the beast and stood with his shoulders pulled back once more. With his sword outstretched in front of him, he moved it to a stone on the top of the pile and brushed it off the beast. Then another. Each stone he brushed off fell to the ground and shattered into hundreds of smaller stones. All thoughts of danger didn't matter to him anymore. He was in the Hallowed Woods, and if his fate was to be torn apart by antlers, then so be it. If he died as a virtuous man, he would be satisfied with that.

He pulled another stone off, and the animal again shook, struggling to escape. Then another. Then another. Finally, the monstrous beast once more raised his leg out of the pile and onto the crumbled stone. Argo stepped back with Wander close behind him. He held the torch and sword in front of him in defense. Wander stayed low to the ground and growled deeply at the creature.

The beast lifted his other front leg from the pile and slowly pried his body from the rubble. The last of the stones rolled off his back and crashed along the ground.

Without even a glance at the two, he shook off the dust and was gone.

CHAPTER 18

The Stream

Argo and Wander watched the creature sprint away alongside the stream until it was soon out of sight. The torch still burned in his hand, its flame trailing the fleeing animal. As soon as it was out of sight, the flame whirled in circles, then came to gently blow back down the stream.

Argo turned and looked at Wander, then knelt and gave her a big hug, relieved that the matter had come and gone so suddenly. His sword shook uncontrollably in his hand. He quickly set it and the torch against the rubble, feeling his grip about to loosen. His fingers ached from holding so tightly. The excitement of the fleeting moment had finally caught up with him. Jitters ran down his spine and into his limbs, and his stomach rumbled and ran cold as if ice were sinking into it. He composed himself as best he could but had to rest the sheath on the ground to slide the sword back in. How embarrassing it would have been had anybody witnessed that he was shaking too much to sheath his own sword.

When the rush had come to settle, Argo went back to the big structure and up the stairs to gather his pack and supplies, which sat precisely where he had left them. He took inventory. "Knife, food, torch… Where's the flintstone?" he asked Wander.

She was standing on the steps and cocked her head at the question.

"The flintstone," he said again. Wander stared at him. He crept over to the edge of the small platform and looked down, careful not to break it. "Got it. It's down there," he said, answering his own question. He threw on his backpack and followed the steps back down.

While picking up the flintstone, something on the stone wall caught his attention. There below the platform was a large image thinly carved into the gray stone bricks. It stood almost as tall as him and had an intricate amount of detail. Argo cleared the sweat out of his eyes and ran his hands across it.

There, carved in front of him, was a poorly-etched but unmistakable image of the Lady of the Woods. Each one of her hairs was diligently carved. Every detail down to her fingernails had been masterfully crafted.

How? Maybe a traveler who knew her passed through here and carved it? Enough people have stayed with her before their journey, so it makes sense they would be thinking about her. This must've taken forever to carve though. Someone must've been living here, but surely without The Rider?

He felt the meticulously cut grooves with his fingertips. A light, weathered coat of moss and grime glazed the image. "This had to have been carved ages ago," he said under his breath. He turned to Wander, who stared at him. Her tongue hung out, and she was panting lightly.

"Let's get out of here, girl," he said, looking back at the carved image of The Lady. She took off and continued sniffing the area. He followed her around the rubble and back to the center of the old stone structures. Her sniffing picked up on the great beast's tracks. Her nose followed him to the stream, then she stopped and looked back at Argo. "You think we should follow this stream?" he asked her. "I do too. Looks like that beast is doing the same."

He trailed behind her and closely examined the heavy tracks that sank slightly into the soft forest soil. Each one was slightly larger than his hand and they were spread widely apart, which even though they saw the beast run off, at least proved that he was running. The stench of grime and filth still lingered in his trail—both of them were familiar enough with tracking to notice it. "Where do you think he went?" he asked Wander. She continued to use her nose along the trail. "Go. Follow it, girl," he told her softly. Despite all the noise earlier, he wanted to get back to staying as quiet and vigilant as possible in case the beast turned around or attacked them again.

The tracks followed a small stream that they crossed and then hand-railed alongside. By this point, the space between them and the beast had narrowed, which showed that the beast had slowed down to an unhurried walk. The muddy path they were now traveling on opened and revealed a decently traveled footpath or small game trail. The grass and foliage gave way in a thin line, which revealed the line of dirt that formed it. An abnormally large tree with a dark, shaded hollow marked the beginning of the trail.

Wander traced this outline excitedly until the gentle stream expanded into a small, perfectly circular pond, no bigger than one of the stone huts. Nothing was around it like with the ponds he'd seen in the past. No weeds, no frogs, no flies. No life at all. It didn't have the usual wet and humid smell of a pond either. The surface was dark and masked everything beneath it. Not even their reflections showed.

Wander followed the beast's tracks straight into the pond. She sniffed at them curiously, then ran around the pond to look for tracks leaving the water. Argo watched her as she circled it, then circled back, her tail wagging excitedly. She did this again and came up with nothing; there seemed to only be tracks leading in, so she stood straight up and carefully approached the water's edge to look into the pond. Her only experience swimming had been from Argo carrying her when he swam.

Argo came up to her and bent down over the tracks. Sure enough, they ran straight into the water. *That's strange. These tracks resemble a boar's closely enough, and boar's usually stick to the mud around water. They never really swim in it though.* He put his torch close to the tracks to give him more light. The flames blew softly toward the water's surface, as if they were kissing it. He stared curiously at them, then stood and circled the pond with Wander. *No exit tracks.*

The flame remained locked on the pond. "What do you make of this, girl?" he asked Wander, who walked beside him as if he had the answer. Argo looked around the forest for clues. It looked the same in all directions: a mirage of moss and trees, as if it were a backdrop painted on a wall. The only break was the small stream coming from the same direction they had come from. It felt as if he were back in the maze.

Argo knelt at the water's edge and searched for tracks beneath the surface, but he saw nothing. He picked up a small stone lying by the stream and tossed it lightly into the pond. It disappeared without a splash, passing through the water as if it weren't there. He stared at the spot where the rock has entered the water, then threw another rock in. Again, it passed through as if the water weren't there. He moved closer, dipped his finger beneath the water's surface, and pulled it out completely dry. Then he moved to the stream they had drunk from earlier and put his finger in its running water. Wet as normal. Curious, and still gripping the torch, he put his left hand in the water, but only deep enough to get his bottom fingers beneath the surface. They stayed completely dry. He reeled back and sat for a moment, confused about what was happening. He slowly placed his foot in the water and didn't feel anything. It felt no different than any other step. Bit by bit, he walked himself into the pond until he was up to his neck. Only his head and hand with the torch remained above the surface.

Wander ran from side to side at the edge of the pond, still watching as curiously as ever. Argo inhaled deeply, then lowered himself beneath the surface. Even with his eyes open, he could barely see anything. The light from the surface hardly carried in. Without thinking, he lowered the torch into the water. The flame kept burning. The light danced off the dirt and grassy walls and illuminated the entrance of a long, dark tunnel leading deeper into the pond. Against all instincts, he opened his mouth to see if he could breathe. It felt eerily normal, so he inhaled and it felt normal as well.

Outside the water, Wander barked loudly. Argo raised his hand out of the water and signaled for her to come in. The barking continued. Knowing she wouldn't come in, he walked back out of the water, picked her up under one arm, and held her tight against his body. She squirmed wildly, trying to escape. He quickly walked back into the water and submerged the two of them. Wander went crazy. She kicked and clawed and broke out of her master's arms. She hit the ground beneath the lake and cowered down, her tail tucked between her legs and her ears down.

"It's okay, it's okay, girl," he explained, trying to comfort her. He leaned down and petted her on her head, "It's okay, girl. We're fine, see?" She picked herself up and clawed at the dirt. Seeing it was normal, she then ran out to the surface and back into the water. He watched her for a moment, then grabbed her when she ran back in, letting out a small laugh. "Come on, girl, let's go down here."

He pointed the torch down the tunnel and the flame whisked toward it lightly. The path opened to a large tunnel of darkness wide enough for two wagons to fit through side by side. The air was humid and musty, and it carried a light-yet-foul odor of mildew. The air had a green tint, as if they were underwater. The light from the flame refracted and looked softer than it normally did on the outside. It lit up the rocky walls of the tunnel and revealed small weeds growing in its crevasses. Wander's excitement faded, and now the two stood in bewilderment at the scene before them. Argo reached down and ran his fingers through her fur, then stepped into the tunnel.

CHAPTER 19

The Tunnel

The sunlit rays of the outside world faded behind them until they were left with only the torchlight. The flame kept pointing them forward as if a strong wind was at their backs, and the flickering light gave the tunnel a strange green ambience. Beyond that lay a pitch-black abyss. The only sound came from the crackling of the torch in Argo's left hand. His sword remained drawn in his right. Both shook from his nerves. He'd never found comfort in tight spaces and much preferred the open air of the forest. Each of his footsteps sank into a soft sand beneath him. It wasn't wet, but it behaved like the soft dirt in the ponds he'd grown up swimming in.

Wander picked up on his nervousness and remained tight by her master's side. Her tail was no longer wagging but drooped low between her legs as she shuffled beside him. She kept her nose close to the ground for any scent that might continue to guide them while Argo swept the torch back and forth from one part of the wall to the next, paying close attention to any sign or hint of direction. Finally, he waved it to the wall on his right and saw that it had opened. The thick air gave way, and he knew the tunnel must have opened to a larger chamber.

Argo's heart skipped a beat when he noticed the flame in his torch whirling wildly in circles. He watched it whip and dance and dreadfully waited for it to settle, but it never did. The torchlight danced across the walls enough to reveal the room they were now in. The long corridor they'd come down had expanded into a massive chamber with four separate chambers to choose from, each one identical to the other. Argo's gut wrenched at the hopelessness of his predicament. He turned to Wander, who ran to each entrance and sniffed the ground, though not daring to leave the safety of the torchlight. He raised the torch to look for any sign or indication of the right tunnel. On the wall above the tunnels read an inscription in the same language shown on his torch and the huts he was in earlier. *I can't read this. I'm not supposed to. It's meant to be like this. To keep people like me from passing.*

He waved the torchlight around and couldn't find any other indications or hints. He bent down and examined the soft sand, but he discovered it to be all the same rugged sand with no sign or tracks to follow. He looked behind him at his own trail, and even that was lost to the earth.

Wander was trotting from corridor to corridor with her nose close to the sand. After each tunnel she visited, she would return to the third tunnel from the left and smell it again. "What is it, Wander?" he whispered loudly. She looked up at him with her ears perked, then trotted over to him and touched her nose to his leg. "Okay, all right, girl, you've got something?" He bent down to her. "I just want to see the other tunnels first, okay?"

He walked over to the first tunnel and waved his torch down it. Nothing but pitch darkness extending as far as his eyes could see, which wasn't more than about ten feet ahead of him. He walked to the second tunnel and this time took a couple steps into it, waving his torch from side to side, paying close attention to the walls and ground. Something far down the tunnel caught his eyes. He squinted and waved the torch again. There it was again, a faint light barely bright enough to make out through the darkness.

"Wander," he whispered loudly. "This way."

Wander stood at the entrance of the tunnel and refused to follow him.

"Come on, girl," he commanded.

Wander lay down in the sand and she stared at her master.

"All right, you stay here for a minute. I'll be right back." He turned and faced the light at the end of the tunnel once again. As he drew near, the light became brighter with each step. It waved and billowed the same as his torch, which was now at full tilt in the direction in which he was heading. He held his sword tightly in his sweaty hand, and he could only hear his heavy breathing through the uncomfortable silence. He took another step closer. The mysterious light did too.

Then another. The light followed.

The figure holding it was still invisible, though through the dim light, he could see an outstretched arm holding it. The image rippled as if he were looking at his reflection on the surface of water.

Argo's heartbeat quickened and the blood from his limbs rushed into his chest. He felt as if he could faint at any moment, but he had to see. He took yet another step closer. This time, he made out long brown hair falling over the shoulder of the figure holding the light across from him. He leaned in closer to make out more and took another step forward.

Now it was clear.

He recognized the figure but couldn't believe it. He took two more steps forward and could see it entirely.

"Mother?" He could barely get the words out as he took another step closer. The invisible barrier between them rippled with his words. It was her, holding the torch across from him. She looked just as she had on the day she'd traveled with The Rider, not a day older.

"Mother?" he asked again, shaking with the word. Again, the image of his mother rippled like water. His sword shook in his hand. His muscles felt weak, and he lowered the sword.

She said nothing, only reached out her hand and took another step closer to him.

Argo felt sick and weak. Tears formed in his eyes, and he lowered his torch. The flame still illuminated the two. "Is this real?" he asked as tears rolled down his cheeks. "Don't do this to me if it's not." He hesitated to put his hand out to hers.

She stared at him with a blank and empty expression. They were only steps apart, separated only by the strange, watery barrier between them.

Woof!

Wander barked from the darkness of the tunnel behind him.

Argo instinctively turned to her and saw nothing. He turned back to face his mother, though she no longer stood in front of him. Instead, he saw himself standing in front of him as his own reflection.

Argo froze in terror.

His reflection had a menacing and sinister horror about him, like a bad, contorted dream. He gritted his teeth in anger and breathed unnaturally, heavily. Between them, the reflection held the torch, its flames clawing towards Argo. He raised his sword and pushed it slowly through the barrier between them, the surface rippling like the sharp point had come out of water. He pinned the blade slowly against The Rider's letter in Argos's breast pocket.

Argo stayed frozen in shock, immobilized by his fear.

Woof!

He snapped out of the trance and looked at Wander, now by his side, growling deeply and thunderously. The white of her sharp teeth reflected off the torchlight.

The terrifying reflection looked down at her.

Woof!

Argo felt a sting in his chest and saw his reflection's sword slowly digging into his breast pocket. The blade punctured through the cloth and The Rider's letter. Blood pooled around the letter.

Argo screamed a deathly cry and threw his sword up, swatting the foreign sword away from him. It cut away at his blouse.

His reflection took the blow and remained standing in place.

"Run!" Argo yelled to Wander as he turned and grabbed her. The two ran with all their strength back down the tunnel. They passed back through the large chamber and turned for a return glance down the tunnel. There, he saw his reflection still standing, sword and torch in hand. Though it was far away now, he could just make out the terrifying grin still marked across his mirrored face.

Wander barked again and was standing in front of the third tunnel. Argo ran over to her, feeling the blood on his chest as he ran. It was just a light cut that had barely broken the skin. Wander ran down the tunnel ahead of her master and circled something on the ground, then lapped it up before he could make it out. She darted down the tunnel, this time going slowly enough for Argo to keep up. The two ran with all their might until they saw a light at the end of the tunnel again. This time, it looked like daylight.

Just before reaching the opening, Wander sniffed and circled something else in the sand. Argo snatched it before she could eat it. It was a broken-off slice of smelly white cheese.

CHAPTER 20

The Valley

Argo and Wander emerged from the pond and found themselves no longer in the mysterious forest. Rocky, gray cliffs towered above them on all sides, taller than anything he'd ever seen before, and it looked like they were standing in depths of a deep valley. The walls were swallowed by old green-gray lichen, which grew in and out of the crevasses. Black and brown streaks of grime trailed beneath these patches that had been discolored from the water.

Argo could barely see the top of the cliffs, and for a moment, he thought they might touch the sky. Long vines strew from the jagged and steep rocky outcroppings. High above, a small rock tumbled down the steep cliffside and bounced off an overhang, then fell several more moments before breaking apart loudly on the ground.

Wander ran from the pond up to the base of the cliff, then immediately to the other side of the pond. She looked back at Argo, then ran around curiously in all directions. She circled the small pond, which sat at the dead end of the valley. She came back to Argo and then she turned and did it again. He normally loved watching her get excited like this, but now he watched with an anxious perplexity of the situation they were in. The sinking feeling had returned to his gut, and shivers ran down his spine and to his fingertips. He traced the outline of the high walls with his eyes and saw birds flying high above them. In front of them was a lowly footpath that traveled down the valley. The torch he still held blew gently down its direction. This was the only possible path they could take aside from retracing their steps through the pond or climbing the impossibly high walls. Argo studied them and knew he could possibly risk climbing them if the need arose, but that would lead to complications on how he'd carry Wander, or whether the vines would stop and leave him stranded on the wall.

He extinguished the torch and knelt to feel the earth. The soil was different here than in the forest—thin and rocky—yet smelled fresh and clean. Tiny herbs and green grass grew from the sides of the path and in between the stones near the walls. The greenery blended seamlessly to the base of the cliffs and up their sides, which served as a testament to the lost and forlorn nature of the place. Next to Wander's paw prints, several other disturbances in the dirt showed that the path was well traveled. Like the tunnel, they were too stirred up to reveal what the exact prints were; nevertheless, it gave him a slight feeling of relief that he wasn't the first to come this way.

Wander ran up to him when he was crouched over and lapped his face. He turned his head and she kept licking. "All right, all right, girl. I love you too," he said, smiling as he petted her head, and he pressed her tightly against him. "Only one way to go from here."

They stood up and cautiously walked down the path. The air was surprisingly fresh and soft. It now felt much lighter than it had in the Woods. The path was jagged and wound through the thick rock like a snake, twisting and bending behind the giant walls. They moved slowly and approached every blind corner just as carefully as the one before. A large shadow passed over Argo's eyes, only for an instant. He immediately stopped and looked up. High above them, small specks buzzed across the sky. They looked like a gaggle of gnats, but they were birds. The valley's walls sloped outward and opened at the top, giving the birds enough room to circle over their heads. They let out loud caws that echoed through the canyon.

"I don't like this, girl," he said to Wander. "I don't like this at all."

Her eyes tracked the birds cautiously. A low growl rumbled deep in her chest.

"We need to keep moving, Wander. Let's get out of here."

They picked up their pace to a quick jog. The walls revealed no more than they had previously. High above, vines strung across the walls and cast thin shadows from the sun. Now even more shadows raced across their path from the birds. The shadows skipped along the walls and, every so often, blotted the sun. At the sight of these, Wander abandoned her scent trail and followed the shadows.

They turned a small curve and ran into another long stretch of canyon. This time, rows of birds were perched on the cliff walls, watching from their perches intently and letting out loud *caws* as the travelers passed. They were crows, black as The Rider himself. Each one seemed half the size of his dog.

"Wander," Argo whispered loudly. "Wander, stay close, girl." He pulled her in. He wanted to explain how the birds were starting to feel threatening, but he held his words out of caution that they might hear and somehow act on it. The two slowed back down to a walk and stayed close together. The numbers of birds grew the farther they went. Before they knew it, the walls were lined with crowds of birds, all watching over the visitors silently.

Caw! Caw!

The calls from the crows broke the still silence and echoed loudly down the walls.

"Stay close, Wander." Argo knelt and dug through his knapsack, digging as calmly as he could for his torch. He pulled it out and struck his flintstone forcefully.

Caw! Caw! Caw!

The calls grew louder.

He struck the stone again, and the sparks flew deafly on the torch. He struck once more, and once more the sparks fell dead.

Caw! Caw! Caw!

Shadows stirred across the path.

Wander looked up and backed up tight against him. Her eyes never left the birds as more of them flew overhead. He struck the rock again and again, and the sparks fell coldly on the torch. The squalls grew louder, and a circle of shadows danced around them, blocking the sun almost entirely. He kept his head down, fixated on the flintstone. Spark after spark flew, but to no result.

Wander gave a low and terrifying growl. Her lips snarled and showed her deathly white fangs. Suddenly, a crow took a dive at her. She leaped defiantly to meet it midair. It pulled back just out of her reach. She snapped her teeth furiously and backed into Argo.

Faster and faster, he struck the flintstone.

Another crow took a dive. Wander leaped remorselessly at it. The bird pulled back out of her reach. She barked fiercely and it echoed through the canyon. The crows matched her energy and cawed even louder. Now the whole valley roared like a massive crowd.

Argo struck once again, and a small ember finally stuck to the torch. Without looking up, he cupped his hand and blew on the glowing light. The small flame grew, then quickly bellowed into its true form. He stood and drew his sword, raising the torch high. He and Wander stood back-to-back in the great valley, carefully watching the crows circle closer over them.

Another crow took a dive. Argo stabbed his sword high at it and struck cleanly. The blade was heavy, and it caught the crow clearly off guard. It fell like a dead weight and flapped its wings rapidly on the ground.

Caw! Caw! Caw!

Wander leaped at another crow and grabbed it savagely in her teeth. They fell to the ground and she tore at it mercilessly. Argo turned and swiped at another crow that dove at them but missed. He and his dog circled together, still at each other's backs. He waved the torch high in front of him to ward off the foes. One of the crows swooped down to steal it but narrowly missed. Argo whipped back sharply, just in time to see another crow dive straight at his face. He quickly raised his sword and felt the blade cut the bird in two. A cloud of black feathers burst in the air. He spun back around and saw a crow biting at Wander's back as she ripped away at another one on the ground.

"Get off!" he yelled, jamming his torch sharply into the bird. He drove it to the ground and pinned it there while the torch still burned, then turned and swiped wildly into the air, striking nothing. Another crow flew directly in his face and flapped its wings brutishly against it, blinding and scratching him in a mess of chaos. Argo screamed and tore the crow away from his face with his sword hand. It fell to the ground without a moment wasted. Wander ripped it away and thrashed at it on the ground.

The birds came in ceaselessly. Argo and Wander yelled and barked and struck wildly at the mess of beasts that were diving senselessly into them. They were now engulfing them in a jet black mass. Something hard hit Argo on the shoulder. He looked up and saw two crows flying away with his knapsack held upside-down, scattering his possessions across the valley. He yelled and struck again, and another bird dropped.

Wander let out a loud cry behind him. A band of crows had dug into her back and were attempting to lift her into the air.

"Wander!" he yelled, fighting his way to her. His voice was lost in the cries of crows. She was hovering low above the ground. She thrashed aggressively, trying to get away from them, her cries drowned out by the horde around her.

Blood and sweat stung Argo's eyes and blinded him. He wiped them off quickly with his sleeve, all while feeling himself being clawed and pecked ruthlessly from behind. Now his cloak lifted behind him as more and more of the flock latched onto it.

The birds sank their claws into Wander and lifted her higher and higher. Argo threw his torch at one of them and missed, then jumped up and grabbed Wander by the leg. He pulled her forcefully back down to the ground and ran his sword along her body to dislodge the birds from her fur. The birds scattered for a second and hovered over them. But then they regrouped and attacked again, pecking and tearing at them both.

Dropping his weight over Wander, he pinned her to the ground, covering her with his body. He reached for his cloak and draped what he could over them both, restraining it down over them with his forearms. The pecking and clawing continued endlessly. More crows joined in. He curled into a ball and dug his face deep into Wander's back. She whined terribly. He closed his eyes and gritted his teeth, pulling even tighter around her. He'd done all he could do.

CHAPTER 21

The Crow

The attack persisted. Their claws dug into Argo's back like razor blades. The cloak pulled in every direction behind him. He kept all his weight on its tucked corners. Through a hole in the corner, he saw the sunlight disappear entirely, covered by the vicious cloud of crows.

Then by some instant and obedient command, the pecking and clawing suddenly stopped. Silence swept through the valley like a gust of wind, and all was quiet. Above them, Argo heard a thick rush and flutter of loud wings. He listened to the deafening silence, though all he could hear was his heart beating through his chest. Beneath him, he felt and heard Wander's do the same.

She heard the new sound the same as him. Her ears perked up and she dug her nose out from beneath the cloak. He cautiously lifted his cloak from where she looked out. Above them, a crow larger than any human rested on a perch in the cliffside. His murder of crows, only a fraction of his size, sat willfully obedient among the valley walls surrounding him. The great creature stared at him then cocked his head to the side and fluttered his large and magnificent wings, which were easily twice, if not triple, Argo's height. The great crow's jet-black feathers' sheen glowed in the sunlight. His beak and legs were entirely black as well. If it had been any less sunny, he would've blended into the cliff as a mere shadow. His uncanny dark and beady eyes stared down at Argo and Wander as if they were divine.

Argo threw back his cloak and crawled quickly to his sword, then stood dutifully toward the leader of crows with the blade drawn in front of him. Wander stood defensively among a mess of birds and feathers next to him. Though she was covered in scratches, she seemed well enough.

"You are different," the magnificent crow said slowly, examining the young man before him.

Argo was even more taken aback than before.

"You've never heard a crow who could speak before, I presume?" The crow's speech was elegant and articulate, full of poise and brilliance.

Argo couldn't find his words. He was covered in blood and dirt, which ran down the side of his face in long beads of sweat. He wiped it away quickly with his sleeve, then held the sword outstretched again.

"What is your name, lad?" the crow asked.

"Ar—it's Argo," he stammered.

"And your dog?"

"Wander."

"Ah… the Brave Argo and his loyal companion Wander," he said proudly. "I heard you were to be expected."

This took Argo aback. "You knew I was coming?" he asked hesitantly.

"Yes. I like to stay informed, if I may. You know, Argo, I was once like you and Wander. Long ago."

Argo gripped the sword in his hand with every muscle tensed.

"Ah, of course." The crow noticed him tense up. "It's all right, young Argo. I won't hurt you or your companion. Please, sit, sit down." With his wing, he indicated for Argo to sit on the rock nearby.

Argo moved to it, keeping his eyes fixated on the beast.

"I suppose I should formally apologize," the crow said. "You're different from the travelers who would normally pass through here. You're…" The giant crow lifted from his perch on a rock face and hopped quickly to a closer one. "You're alive, aren't you?" The crow leaned in as he spoke the words. His eyes widened, and he cocked his head again to the side. "You see, this is almost as much of a shock to me as it is for you to be talking to a crow."

Argo stared at him, unsure of where the conversation would lead.

"Well, I suppose I should explain then. My name is Silas. My murder doesn't normally attack travelers along this path, you see, as this path is only traveled by those escorted by The Rider. Those who are in the process, if you will, of dying, passing to the afterlife. This being the case, those travelers no longer have need of their possessions. Thus, my murder is positioned precisely here at this point to see to it that those possessions remain behind."

The crow paced slowly back and forth on his perch as he spoke. "Now, I submit that my murder did provoke an attack, and I hope you understand, given the nature of this path and the need of our profession, that it was of no ill will." He bowed his head, giving Argo the impression that he might be apologizing. "Furthermore, I have yet to understand the events that have led you and your loyal companion here; however, I recognize the cause of your confusion, and I forgive you for killing some of my own while acting in your own defense." The crow stopped pacing and looked at Argo. "Now, I imagine you are experiencing a number of emotions of your own, so please, when you are ready, you may ask any questions you may have." He fluffed his feathers, then let them come to rest.

Argo sat staring in awe, taking in the great crow's words and absorbing them the best he could, then mustered all the nerves and few words he could. "Thank you." His hands shook wildly from the comedown of adrenaline. He stuck his sword into a patch of soft dirt as best he could. It hit a rock, but the blade held in the ground nonetheless. He was unsure how to feel, and despite Silas's efforts of comforting him, he couldn't shake the thought that the great beast could pick both of them clean at any moment.

"You said you were once like us?" he humbly asked, voicing the first thought that came to his mind. His voice trembled and sounded less of a young man than he had hoped.

"Alive, yes. Not just in this strange land either," he replied.

"What happened?" Argo asked, relaxing his guard.

"I was slain," he said, "long ago, by a great man. This was in the time before The Rider. You see, I was a great creature. There are, and were, no others like me. I flew high above the forests and did my best to always mind my own. Though, when you're my size, it's rather difficult to go unnoticed. I had flown across the world and saw many great sights and hunted in many great lands. Never for your kind though. Word of me spread to all corners of the land, and before I knew it, men in pursuit of greatness sought me as a trophy." He turned and paced on his ledge again, which was a small flat area of rock in the cliffside.

"Do you know the paradox of men seeking greatness?" he continued. "It comes at the expense of great things." Silas paused another moment. "So, I stopped flying. I tucked myself away in the forest. The more I ran and hid, the more men sought me. The more elusive I tried to be, the more of a challenge I became. When they did eventually find me, I fought back. I hated it. I hated every second of it. I didn't want to fight. It wasn't me. The more I fought, the greater man's ambition grew. Thus, the paradox of it all wound even tighter. Now at this point, they wanted a fight. They wanted a tale so great that their song would be sung long after their time." He stopped pacing and looked up the footpath toward the pond. "And they wanted it from me."

The story struck a nerve with Argo. He felt a deep-seated guilt in his soul. He was no better than the men Silas spoke of. The reflection from his words was as clear as any mirror, and in them, Argo saw the pain of his own greed and ambition. *Mine's different though. Right? I don't want to hurt anything. It's not me either.* He looked at the mess of crows lying in pieces on the ground and felt a deep and painful irony. "What happened?" he asked Silas.

"Ah, one day a truly great man found me. He was armed with a rather sizable broadsword and rode atop a horse larger than any I'd ever seen before. Just as I was descending upon him, fully intending to end him, the man laid down his arms, right there on the ground in front of me. I was dumbfounded, to say the least. I could have snatched him up and cleaned him, same as the ones before. But I was curious."

Silas hopped to another ledge beside him. As he spoke, he stretched out his wings and gestured as best he could. "The man introduced himself, then emptied his knapsack in front of me. Strewn across the ground were strange vegetables and meats that he'd gathered from across the land. Frogs, rabbits, foxes, carrots, you name it. He gave me everything I once cherished from my own travels. Then he set up camp, and we shared a meal. He was the first person I ever got to have a conversation with, Argo."

"And then what happened?" He'd become so enthralled in the story that the words came out almost instinctively.

"Well, after the meal, the traveler explained that he was heading west. He invited me to join, and I agreed."

"And you ended up here?" Argo asked.

"We ended up in many places," he replied.

"How'd you end up here?" Argo asked eagerly.

"I was slain."

"By whom? The man?" he pressed.

"No." Silas gave a small laugh. "I was slain by the greatest force of them all, Argo. Time."

Argo stayed silent.

"I saw how you looked at them. My crows." Silas signaled to the bodies of the slain crows on the ground. "It's all right, dear boy. They haven't much wit, but they understand."

"I'm sorry, Silas," Argo confessed, feeling guilty despite the truth in Silas's words. "I never wanted to hurt them either. I don't like hurting anything." He was no stranger to killing, but it felt different this time. Speaking with Silas made him feel like the birds were something more than what they were. "It seems like lately, killing is all I've been doing."

"No, no," Silas comforted him. "I know you didn't want to kill them. Such is life, Argo. We don't get the luxury of deciding the actions of others. My crows would have killed you and dear Wander had you not killed them first. It's quite simple really. Do not pity those who fall within their nature."

"I suppose. I'm glad you see it that way. I feel awful. About everything, really." He kicked at one of the rocks on the ground as he spoke, not wanting to look up. "The more I travel on this journey, the more it seems like the right thing to do is nothing at all. I should've stayed home and wasted my days away. It seems like all I ever do is hurt others, whether I mean to or not. Despite the boar I killed the other day, and your crows, I feel as if I've hurt my friends and father by coming here." He flipped another rock over with his foot, too ashamed of himself to look up at the great crow.

"Argo." Silas looked at him reassuringly. "You're young. There's wisdom in this world that only comes through experiences such as those. Let the pain and emotions sink in. Feel them." Silas let his words resonate. "You're a good, young man, and no good, young man wants to cause suffering. But you're also a wise man, and wise men know that suffering is inevitable. It's in all life, and it's necessary for all growth."

Argo thought about this for a moment, still kicking the rocks at his feet. Wander had fallen fast asleep at his side. Despite the dried blood in her fur, she appeared fine and not seriously injured. "You're right," he admitted. "I just hate being the cause of pain. I was only trying to do something that I thought was right."

"This goes deeper than my crows, I'm sure." Silas nodded. "Argo, you cannot take on the pain of others. A man's soul can only bear so much weight." He paused again, then jumped to another perch close by. "As I recall, when I used to hunt for a fox, I would undoubtedly cause a tragic event for the poor fellow. However, it was necessary for me to survive. It was inevitable. When the fox hunted rabbits, the same could be said for them as well. And so the cycle goes. One depends on the other to live, so to speak. Despite our primal intentions of wanting to eat, I would kill with no ill will toward my prey, and I would assume the fox would feel the same. The same applies to you now, Argo. While there's still much to be discussed about this quest you're on, I assume that you undertook this challenge because it was necessary for you to survive, just like hunting is for myself and the fox. And I recall, you said that you felt you were trying to do something right, correct?"

Argo finally looked up at Silas and shook his head.

"What's right for one may not be right for all," Silas said, "and what's right for all may not be right for one. I never asked the fox's opinion on being eaten."

Argo thought back to his time at the village. He remembered the conversations with Abaddon, Emeric, Castor, his father, and even the Lady. If he'd only told his father and the Lady, he would've felt completely justified in his quest, but he hadn't. He'd told his friends and they had told the village, and now everyone disagreed wholeheartedly with the manner.

Argo dug through his breast pocket and pulled out The Rider's letter. The parchment was bloodied and beaten from the journey. "This is why I'm here, being alive and all. This is why."

"Ah." Silas observed the letter in his hands. "And how many days remain?"

"Three."

"Hm. Well, I say, you are the first I've seen to arrive early, not to mention on your own accord as well."

"I received the letter three days ago. I…" Argo paused for a moment to articulate his point, then it all came rushing out of him. "I was so tired, maybe even frustrated, seeing people waste away as they were. I saw it worse than any fate, and I couldn't stand it. I decided to come into the Woods and meet The Rider myself. Originally, I wanted to find him and challenge him. I wanted to make a journey and make the fight worthy of a great story. I wanted to be a hero. Now, the more I travel and the deeper into the Woods I go, the less clear all of that is to me." He sat back down almost defeatedly. "I don't feel like a hero. I feel blind. Lost even. And now after hearing your story and how men sought to hunt you down, I feel even worse." He looked to his side. "I worry for Wander as well. She's come with me on this quest where my fate is decided and hers is so undecided. She's my best friend, and I love her more than I love myself. I fear what may become of her."

"I see… Such is the cycle of life, Argo. I understand your attachment to this quest. Do you?"

Argo thought once more. "I … I don't know. Maybe it's to be remembered?"

"What's so important about being remembered?" he asked.

"What else is there?" Argo answered.

Silas didn't answer but instead nodded slowly in agreement, then scratched his face with his wings. "Over time, heroes turn to legends, and legends fade into myths. There is a beginning and end to all things. The finality of it all is rather lovely."

"Not when it's the end of something you love," Argo replied.

"No, not when it's something you love." Silas's words drifted off quietly. He fluttered his great wings once more and leaped to another perch. This one was an old tree limb growing from the cliffside. The limb bent under his weight and bounced up and down slowly as Silas settled his weight.

"Notice this perch that I'm on, Argo," he said. "This is actually my favorite perch, and I'm not just saying that. Can you imagine why I love this perch so much?"

"Why?" Argo asked innocently.

"Well, I love everything about this perch. I love the way it bends and sways, and how it sits at this unique position to observe this valley. But most of all, I love how fragile it is. I love how it can break under me at any moment, and if it weren't for my gift of flight, it could send me tumbling down to the ground below. Now, to me, I see this perch as already having been broken. I see it as fallen to the ground and broken into pieces. In this view, I've come to appreciate every moment with this branch not yet broken. Knowing that this branch will not last forever gives me a greater appreciation for the time I have to enjoy it."

Argo sat back and let himself absorb Silas's words, as he had once done with the Lady's teachings. The story flew gracefully and landed on his heart like a heavy weight. He scratched Wander behind her ears. She squinted her eyes a little harder as she slept, deep in a dream, and her beat-up paws flinched as if she were running. He felt a troublesome worry as he petted her. "It makes sense. It does. So, is it a blessing or a curse?" he asked Silas. "This life."

"Ah, young Argo. That depends on how you live it."

As they spoke, the sun crept steadily down the sky until it lay perfectly in the basket of the valley. Bright colors filled the sky in a beautiful array.

"Night will be coming soon," Silas said as he bounced slowly up and down on his branch. "Rest here, Brave Argo. You and Wander will need your strength for the path ahead. Feast on my crows for dinner. It won't be much, granted; however, they have no further need for their bodies, and I'm sure we would all prefer it if they didn't go to waste." Then he turned to his audience of crows and gave a series of loud clicks from his beak.

Waves of crows immediately took flight, once again blocking out the sun momentarily.

"Firewood is scarce in this valley," Silas said. "They'll bring you some. I'll see you in the morning at first light," he reassured him, watching his crows fly off into the distance. "I rather enjoyed our conversation and would much prefer to speak once again before you set off. Goodnight, you two." And with that, the great crow opened his tremendous wings. Before he flew off, he pecked at the base of his favorite perch with a powerful strike. The branch split loudly and tumbled to the ground below, where it broke into pieces.

"For your fire," the crow remarked before flying high above the canyon walls.

CHAPTER 22

The Friend

Night came smoothly. Argo rinsed his and Wander's plentiful wounds with water from his waterskins and found them to be only minor scratches. Afterwards, as he had done on the previous nights, he stared into the flames and reflected on all things that needed reflection. He fell back and lay with his head resting on Wander, and he gazed at the narrow-yet-vast array of stars overhead that seemed to pass over the valley with careless ease. They made him feel small, and while his quest was without a doubt the crescendo of his life, he felt that it paled in comparison to the mysteries around him.

The still silence of the night brought forth the questions he'd been too occupied to ask before. *How could we walk into a pond and stay completely dry? Where were we? Is this still the same world?*

How did the magic work? Was there magic elsewhere?

What's above the valley walls? Where does the valley begin and where does the forest end? Are we even in the forest? Or some part of it?

These thoughts made Argo feel even smaller and possibly even more meaningless. He closed his eyes and imagined himself floating down a river, with the current and rapids taking him for a ride as he calmly lay still. He knew not where the road led, but he knew he was on it.

The morning sunlight poured gracefully into the valley and slowly unveiled the colossal walls once again. Argo and Wander awoke next to a mountain of sticks, logs, and other wooden oddities that the crows had brought for them. In a smaller pile next to this were the supplies and knapsack they had flown away with.

Argo rolled awake and restoked the embers from the coals, which caught the small twigs easily enough to reheat some of the crow meat from the night before. He picked at it delicately and gave some to Wander, who immediately and indiscriminately had her fill and then sat and stared at Argo until he gave her more. He reluctantly did, and she grabbed a piece from his hands and carried it to a soft spot on the grass, then placed it between her paws and picked every scrap of meat from the bones. When she finished picking at it, she came back to sit and stare at Argo once again.

The crows cawed and went about their assumed usual routine. Despite the comfort, Wander remained hyperalert with each sudden movement from the murder. After they finished eating, Argo dug a small hole in the soil between a couple of big rocks and neatly piled the discarded remains of the crows inside. Then he pushed the loose dirt back over them and patted it down.

"No," he told Wander, who was staring at the remains. "Leave it alone." To make sure she didn't dig it up, he moved one of the heavy rocks on top.

Silas flew down from high above the walls, his outspread figure gliding gracefully and casting a considerable shadow across the span of the valley, until he came to rest on the ground, taking his seat near the fire. Argo greeted him kindly.

"Ah, quite a lovely morning," Silas said. His sudden arrival scared Wander, though once she saw how calm her master was, she cautiously approached Silas and sniffed at him. She pulled closer and closer with each sniff, until she felt comfortable enough to relax.

Silas watched her carefully, evidently to show her that he was friendly and meant no harm.

Within moments, Wander dropped low to the ground and wagged her tail excitedly in the air. She sprinted around Silas and the campfire playfully while the others watched merrily.

"You slept all right, I presume?" Silas asked after Wander tired out.

"I did. Thanks for allowing us to stay," Argo responded.

"Yes, yes, of course. Under the right conditions, these walls can be quite comforting," Silas said.

Argo agreed. "Wander and I fell asleep watching the stars last night. It was great to finally feel some peace since being here."

"Ah yes, I can imagine. The view from atop these walls is incredible," Silas replied.

"Silas, I never asked you yesterday... You said you knew I would be coming. How?" Argo asked as he added some thin twigs to the fire.

"Of course, I did mention that. Well, I am terribly sorry, Argo. Your friend passed through here," Silas answered. "Just yesterday, actually, sometime before you arrived."

"Friend?" Argo asked, curious and now suddenly full of dread. "Who was it? What was their name?"

The crow stroked his beak with his foot. "Ah, Emeric, I'm afraid," Silas answered. "He had a dreadful wound in his leg that was festering from infection. I doubt he was able to walk outside these woods much."

Argo immediately thought back to the cheese left in the tunnels. It had been Emeric's. He might've known Argo and Wander would pass through the tunnels, and so Emeric had left them clues. Argo leaned back in remorse. He wiped his hands across his face at the thought of losing his friend. "It's my fault." He shook his head and tucked it between his hands. "He fell from a tree and injured it on a hunt that I took him on. He wasn't ready, but I brought him anyway." He felt dreadful, yet he wasn't crying as he normally would be.

"Well, you can't blame yourself for that, can you? Fate is fate, Argo," the great crow responded.

It all weighed heavily on Argo, yet now he didn't feel so alone. In a strange way, he felt that there were other pieces in motion. He reflected on the news, surprised that the wound on Emeric's leg had flared up, but the news still stung him all the same. "Was he all right? Or in pain?" Argo asked as he poked at the fire with another stick.

"Not in here. Not in these woods," Silas answered.

Argo nodded in understanding. "Was he with The Rider?" he asked, remembering his quest.

"Yes. He was with The Rider," the great crow answered.

Argo nodded slowly with the information. The thought of his friend and The Rider seemed unreal, like they were just within reach and yet so far out of grasp. "He must've received his letter after I left, then met with The Rider that night and passed by here. I must've been right by them that first night. I can't be too far off now." Argo paused. "I'm on the right path then?"

"Depends on where you're trying to go."

"Where The Rider is, I suppose."

"Then you're on the right path," the crow answered.

Argo felt an odd reassurance. "Silas, what can you tell me about The Rider? Do you know him?"

"Ah, I do. I do know him. Very well, as a matter of fact."

Argo waited patiently for Silas to keep speaking, but he'd stopped there. "And who is he? What is he? What can you tell me about him?"

Silas looked hopefully at him. "I can't tell you much. He's just a man, is all. A man who does what he thinks is right."

Argo didn't want to forcefully pry and make his new friend uncomfortable. He could tell that it was a delicate subject for Silas and could feel a tension and uneasiness in his answer.

"That's all I will tell you. It is your quest, after all," Silas told him almost proudly. "Some answers man must unveil on his own."

Argo didn't like the answer, but he understood its meaning. The conversation fell still, and the two stared into the small fire between them. "What is this place? One moment Wander and I were in the Woods, then we went down a strange pond and tunnels and…" Argo stopped himself, thinking back to what had happened in the tunnels. "…then something even more strange happened."

"Well, go on," the crow said. "Let's hear it."

Argo started from when he entered the Hallowed Woods and continued in detail.

"Ah, yes, it is all rather peculiar, isn't it?" Silas said. "I don't quite know anything about the figure in the tunnels, yet the mystery of it all doesn't surprise me. However, those eyes you saw in the darkness, I have an inclination of whom it may be. He's a rather… interesting fellow."

"You know him? And it's a person?" he asked. He stopped poking the fire and held the stick firmly in his hand.

"Yes, I know him. Know of him, I should say." The great crow hopped closer to Argo, as if not to be overheard, and leaned in close. "He calls himself *the Tree Traveler*." His words trailed off as he said the name. He leaned back after saying it. "He's a kid. And quite mad, really, from what I've heard. I've never actually met him though."

"The Tree Traveler…" Argo repeated under his breath. "And what does he want? Why was he watching us?" he asked, his tone as low as Silas's.

"I can't say. I don't know." He shook his beak and ruffled his feathers. They puffed up and settled back down smoothly. "As I understand it, he uses tree hollows as some sort of doorway, I suppose. Uses them to move between places rather quickly. That's all I know of him. Just be wary of any hollows you may come across, Argo."

He slowly nodded in understanding and rested his arms across his knees. Then he turned to Wander, who was stirring in her dream. "We really are in a strange land, girl," he told her as he gently petted her.

"None of this makes sense. What is this place?" he asked the great crow.

"Well to be frank with you, Argo, I can't answer that either, for no other reason than not knowing the answer myself."

The crow's response surprised him.

"That's the interesting thing about us," Silas continued. "We seek explanations and answers for everything. Everything must have a reason or follow a certain set of rules. It has to make some sort of sense, doesn't it? This world isn't like that. There are those who find beauty in the search for these answers, as I often do. But now, maybe in my old age and wisdom, I have grown in deep appreciation for the questions left unanswered. Sometimes you spend your whole life searching for an answer when it's something you don't really want to know." He sighed. "I think about this rather frequently. Now, allow me to ask you something."

Argo agreed.

"Where does the sun come from?" Silas asked.

Argo thought for a moment. "From the east, I suppose."

"Yes, yes, we know it rises in the east, but where does it come from? How did it start?"

"I don't know," Argo responded, "I can't answer that."

"Precisely." The great crow scratched himself with his foot as he spoke. "Yet we take comfort in knowing that it's there, and we know as sure as the day is long that the sun will continue to be there. We've accepted the idea of something we don't fully understand."

Argo agreed once again.

"I like to think life is like that, that this strange land I now consider to be my home is similar in that regard. I can't answer why the sun rises or what have you, but I can tell you that it does. I can't answer how this world works, and to be honest with you, Argo, I don't suppose I want to know. I rather enjoy the mystery of it all."

Argo listened curiously and agreed with Silas's point. The two continued to converse, and together they discussed Argo's parents, the past life in the living world, and much of the small talk that comprises conversation. He could see that Silas took a great appreciation from the dialogue and longed for the genuine connection of good company.

Argo asked if he recalled seeing his mother pass through here years ago, but the effort was in vain. He said he had seen many come and go, and he held no particular memory of any of them. Argo didn't appreciate how his mother was just another passing face, but he understood. Then the conversation progressed, and Argo spoke of his longing of stories and of his time spent enthralled in tales shared by the Lady of the Woods.

"Ah, Adonillis..." Silas mumbled when he heard Argo speak of him. "The Great Hero Adonillis, is it?"

"Yes, you've heard of him as well?" Argo was surprised at this.

"I knew him. He's a good man"

Argo couldn't believe it. "He's real?" he asked in astonishment. "I've heard of him only in tales. He's the only one we speak of." He tried to contain his curiosity. "Is it true that arrows can never hit him? I've heard that he never received a single cut in battle."

Silas laughed at the prospect. "He's quite real, Argo," he said cheerfully. "Adonillis was brave, I will attest. But remember this, Brave Argo," Silas said, reaching out and placed his wing over Argo's shoulder. "True bravery comes from absolute vulnerability." He paused to let the words resonate.

"True bravery comes from absolute vulnerability," Silas repeated. "Could Adonillis be truly brave if he never feared arrows piercing him? Or by knowing he wouldn't be cut? No. Let me tell you something surprising, Argo. It was Adonillis who approached me in the Woods that day. It was he who brought me food and shared his meal with me. That was brave. Braver than the men who came at me with spears and arrows, I'll tell you that." Silas gazed off into the distance.

Argo could hear the sincerity and appreciation in his tone.

"Our time together now is nearing its end, Argo. You and Wander have your grand journey ahead of you. The day is young, and you two have quite a path to travel. Please, let me leave you with this." His wing was still over Argo. He shifted his poise away from the fire, which they had huddled around during their conversation, and faced Argo. His colossal size towered over Argo, and while not threatening, the crow still made him feel small and weak by comparison. "You need not travel into the Woods to meet death. Death comes for us all, whether we sit in our homes or leave them for some grand adventure. The process of dying is called life. Live yours true and live it how you see fit. Fear not of Wander. She knows no other life than the one by your side. Fate takes us all. Fear not of it either, but instead greet it as an old friend. Do this, and you will truly live, dear boy."

Argo nodded once more, then stood to part ways with his new friend. "Farewell, great Silas. We'll see you when we see you."

With that, the great Silas spread his magnificent wings and lifted himself once more into the air, his wings sweeping strong gusts of wind as he flew high and out of the valley. A trail of crows followed in his wake, and Wander and Argo were once again left alone in the colossal valley.

CHAPTER 23

The Hollow

Wander and Argo drifted down the valley like leaves in a stream. They wound through the high cliffs which never ceased in their grandeur. After hours of walking, they turned one of the slight corners of the valley to find the walls had abruptly ended, opening to a forest similar to the one they'd begun their journey in. The high walls loomed overhead in their unbelievable size and jutted out endlessly in both directions from their walkway.

Argo peered along the wall to his left and found it spanning ominously past his view and over the horizon. He tracked the wall upward and barely made out birds flying overhead. They were so high above them now that the birds looked like small moving stars against the drab, cloud-ridden sky. The wall on the other side looked like a mirror image of the first side.

"It looks like we might get some rain here soon, girl," he called to Wander, who was running around and exploring the new scenery. She came to him and lapped at his face happily. Argo, in return, gave her a strong kiss on her forehead, right between her eyes, and pressed his head against hers. "Yesterday was a crazy day," he said after a moment. "Only two days left now. Let's hope these go smoother." He held her close and gave her another kiss. She stood looking at him, still panting from her excitement.

The path from the mouth of the valley continued down a small slope and into the foods. This came as a relief because to this point, Argo had merely been lucky in finding their way. Before stepping away from the safety of the valley walls,

Argo heard a small stream of water that ran quaintly through a small groove it had carved out in the ground. Argo followed it closely and noticed it met up with other small grooves that also cut through the forest floor.

"It must be raining over the valley right now. That's where this water's coming from," he told Wander in a soft voice. Wander trotted over to the stream and lapped up some of the water. Then she rolled over onto her back, tossing and turning in the shallow water, her tail wagging excitedly.

The two continued to walk downstream and deeper into the forest, which now looked identical to the one they were in before. The air was still and quiet, yet it screamed of the calm before a storm. A wistful wind blew softly yet silently toward them as they walked, carrying the scent of far-off rain with it. The sounds of ambient life which usually filled the forest were missing. The trees loomed over them and cast a thick awning of leaves and branches overhead, effectively blotting out the overcast clouds.

As they followed the stream, which now grew to a respectable size, Argo watched Wander run and play cheerfully around it. His heart held such an admiration for his friend, who even now in an unknown and mysterious place, still found happiness and joy in the simple pleasures of life. He'd held her in the highest regard since she was first carried into the village as a puppy. A lone traveler had brought her on his journey from the far east. He'd pulled the litter in a small cart behind him. He was on his way to meet with The Rider and wanted to give away the pups as he passed through the land. Wander was the last puppy. When the man called out that he had one more left, Argo ran up to the cart and saw her resting alone in the cart. At the sight of him, her tail wagged so hard that it also wagged her hind end with each wave.

Argo knew at that point that their two souls had been tied together. The walls he'd placed around his heart from hunting and avoiding attachment to the world had been instantly leveled by this innocent creature in a cart. Since then, he'd do anything for her, and the fact that she was seen by most as just a dog only made that affection stronger. Despite the troubles in the world, Wander had always been a beacon of hope in a life he saw as drab and dull. She was a lantern in the fog and the light in his eyes. Words would do no justice in describing his feelings unless they spilled out in poetry.

Now, in the thick of this strange land, she jumped from one side of the stream to the next, as innocent as the day she was born. The sight amused Argo, and he was thankful to see it breaking up the monotony of the forest.

Together they followed the stream down the gradual slope of the forest floor, winding in and out of the massive trees. In several places, Argo stopped and touched the water to make sure it was real and not like the last pond they'd entered. He didn't know what he was expecting, but it seemed like a reasonable action to take, given the nature of the forest. The stream grew wider and wider until it had formed a small river. Wander stopped jumping across it and trotted happily alongside Argo, who maintained his course on the remnants of the footpath.

A fat raindrop fell and hit Argo right on his nose. *Here it comes.*

Thick splashed of rain started falling faster upon them. "Come here, girl!" he called out to Wander, who stopped in her tracks and looked at her master and then excitedly ran over to him. He grabbed her and held her close to him, then threw the hood of his cloak over his head and wrapped the edges over his shoulders and around his body. He looked at the canopy high above him, but he couldn't make out any of the sky.

"Let's find some cover, girl. I'm not sure how long this will last!" he said loudly over the sound of pouring rain, which now fell on them in sheets. He held her close and ran cautiously down the path. The stream beside them now rushed with water, and the mud sank heavily beneath each step he took. The river was the only means of keeping direction at this point. As they ran, he looked desperately in all directions for some means of cover, but everything around them was shrouded in a mask of heavy rain and thick trees.

"There!" he pointed out to Wander. Beside the raging stream was a large tree with overgrown roots. The soil must've been carved out at some point in time had revealed a web of roots he and Wander could use for cover. Fortunately, the tree was high enough away from the riverbank to not be swept away or further eroded from the rain.

They ran desperately toward it and discovered it was barely large enough to house them both. Argo shoved Wander in first against the tree, then shuffled himself in. His sword stuck into the ground when he leaned over. He pushed it aside and threw his knapsack off. The root den smelled of old musty dirt and fungus mixed with the cooling odor of the relentless rain. He dug through his pack and pulled out the torch and his flintstone, then struck at it until he drew a flame. The warmth and smell of the burning torch gave him great comfort, despite Argo's soaking-wet clothes sticking to him. The flames circled wildly and then came to settle. Suddenly, the flame ripped outside their root cave and blew directly across the rushing river, as if a strong wind were behind it.

Argo stared at the flame; he'd never seen it pull this hard. He gazed over the burning torch and saw that it was bellowing toward a tree no more than a stone's throw away from them. It swayed and blurred from the rising heat of the torch, which he moved to the side and looked at the tree again, this time seeing what it was pointing to.

In the middle of the large tree was a dark hollow as wide and tall as a door. Even through the rain, he could make out its dark shadow against the tree bark. Now he understood.

There, in the middle of the hollow, was a pair of eyes staring back at him.

CHAPTER 24

The Traveler

The eyes pierced through the pouring rain.

Argo met his eyes and slowly pulled his bow and quiver from his pack. *I'm tired of these games. Leave. Us. Alone.*

The eyes across the river blinked. Then they vanished back into the shadow of the hollow.

"Get ready, girl," he said calmly to Wander, who was still tucked tightly away between her master and the back of their root cave. Argo stared at the hollow and waited. Then he heard light footsteps running through the muddy forest floor just outside their cover. He cocked his head to the side to listen.

Out of nowhere, a boy only a few years younger than himself grabbed the torch right out of his hands. He was barefoot and wore brown tattered pants and no shirt. On his dirty blonde head, he wore a wreath of vines. The boy was quick, and the torch slipped out of Argo's grip and in a flash was gone. The young boy ran down the hill along the stream.

Argo immediately crawled out of the root cave to follow him. "Give that back!" he yelled after him. Wander rushed out of the root den behind him and barked wildly. They both took off after the boy. Wander sped ahead.

Argo could see the light of the torch through the pouring rain, which beat down upon them in sheets, but trailed behind the boy with his bow and quiver still in his hands. His pack, though tight to his back, swung from side to side clumsily as they ran.

When Wander got near the boy, he saw her then immediately cut left, away from the flooded stream. Wander swiped hard left after him. Argo saw this and redirected through the forest as a shortcut, keeping his eyes locked on the boy. As he did so, he strapped his quiver to his belt loop. Surprisingly, the distance between them was getting closer.

Then the boy ran at full speed straight toward a tree and ran through its hollow as if the tree were never there at all. Then he was gone.

Wander stopped at the tree and barked furiously. Argo ran up and, without stopping, picked her up and pushed them both into the hollow behind the boy. They were now inside the tree. It was completely black in almost all directions. Behind him was the rainy forest. In front of them was a second hollow opening the same size as the first, except in this one, the forest was completely normal. Argo pushed them both through the second hollow and into the normal, dry forest. It looked identical to the forest they were used to. There, the young boy was resting against one of the trees and holding the torch. Beneath him was a small game path next to a stream.

He looked at them both with wide eyes, taken completely by surprise that he'd been followed. He immediately ran off down the forest path. They took off after him; this time Wander staying close to her master. The boy ran behind a massive tree trunk and jumped through another tree hollow, disappearing again.

They ran after him and jumped through the same hollow, hot on his trail. Unlike before, they didn't stop in the tree but ran through it without any caution. They stumbled out into a forest blanketed with snow. Argo hit a pile of it as he ran out and tripped over it, tumbling through the cold powder. The icy snow stuck to Argo's wet clothes as he stood to his feet.

Footprints.

He followed them down the all-white forest slope and saw the boy jump through another tree hollow in the distance. They followed and jumped through behind him.

A roaring wind blasted on the far-side opening of the hollow. Argo ran to it and stuck his head out. Brown and tan leaves rushed by them madly in a chilly wind which whipped and roared monstrously. Through them, he saw the young boy fighting to run through the fierce gusts, running at a near impossible angle to his side as he fought against it. With one hand he held the torch and with the other he held the ground, trying desperately not to fly over.

"Come on, girl!" Argo yelled to Wander over the wind. They sprinted out of the hollow and were immediately hit by wind as powerful as a river. Argo's pack caught a gust and whipped him over to his side. He tumbled over himself and was swept up by the heavy gale, now sliding over the forest floor.

Woof!

The young boy looked back at them, then kept clawing forward.

Wander ran over to Argo and bit the pack, then planted her feet firmly in the dirt, stopping him from sliding. He dug his hands into the roots and pulled himself back up, standing nearly sideways against that wind. Without saying anything, he held on to Wander as they fought their way forward. Leaves smacked against his face and stung when they hit him. They could still see the young boy ahead as he pulled himself into another hollow and disappeared.

Argo gritted his teeth and continued forward. Above them, a deafening crack tore through the air. They both looked up and saw an enormous branch split apart from a tree upwind from them. It spun and whipped about wildly, hanging on by the thread of its bark. Finally, in a loud crack, it tore from the tree. The wind immediately carried it, spinning it erratically as it tumbled directly toward them. Argo quickly rolled to his side away from it and pulled Wander with him.

The branch slammed the ground ahead of them and tore up earth as it impacted. Just as quickly as it had come, it was gone. Wasting no time, they picked themselves up and clawed their way toward the hollow, throwing themselves inside as quickly as they could.

This time, they were no longer in a forest. Instead, they were high up on a plateau of some kind with clear and empty skies above them, except for a few crows in the distance. The land was flat as far as their eyes could see, except for a handful of leafless, barren trees scattered across the plain. They were small and looked dead, but he could see a dark hollow in one of the trees in the distance. A chilling wind swept across the plain and hit them head on, cutting through his wet clothes like ice.

Ahead of them, he saw the young boy running desperately across the plain toward a tree off in the distance.

"Go, Wander! We need that torch!"

She took off at a dead sprint toward the young boy. Argo ran desperately after them. His heart raced in his chest, and he could see that the boy was equally as tired as himself. Even Wander seemed slower than her usual self. As all three drew closer to the tree, the distance between them began to close. The young boy's running grew sloppy. His arms flailed at his side, and he held the torch lazily downward as he ran. Beside them was a large and deep crevasse in the plain, and it immediately became clear to Argo where they were.

We're on top of the valley.

The young boy was nearly at the tree hollow and Wander quickly closed in behind him. He finally made it and launched himself through. Wander jumped in after him.

Just as Argo was about to rush in as well, he saw the great crow, Silas, flying far behind the tree. All around him were his murder of crows, which moved like a black cloud against the bright blue sky. Then he jumped recklessly through the hollow after the boy.

Now they were back in a normal forest. In front of him, the boy lay flat against the ground with his hands over his head. Wander circled him and barked loudly.

He ran up and saw that she wasn't barking at him; she was barking at the torch the boy had accidentally thrown ahead of him when he fell. It had landed on a bed of leaves and its flame had begun burning into a raging wildfire.

"We need to get out of here!" he called out to the boy and Wander.

The boy looked up and stared fearfully at the growing flames. He picked himself up and scuttled backward on the ground toward Argo, never once taking his eyes off the destruction.

Argo immediately ran past him and toward the torch. The flames had picked up around it, but not completely. One side of the bed was still unlit enough for him to possibly reach it. He ran and jumped over some of the flames to the unlit side. The torch was completely engulfed in the flame. Thinking quickly, he wrapped his hand around the tail end of his soaking-wet cloak, reached into the fire, and grabbed the torch. Even through the cloak, he felt the heat. He quickly tossed it out of the flames and onto a dirt patch by one of the trees. Then he swiftly ran over to it and readjusted his grip and grabbed it again. Already, it had significantly cooled down.

He looked back at Wander and the young boy who were both terrified and watching the destruction grow. Now, the flames had taken off down the forest and crawled up the trees. The smell of charred grass and roots filled the forest with a deathly gray smoke. Argo ran over to the young boy, still petrified on the ground, and shouted, "We need a way out of here!"

The boy couldn't speak. His eyes were fixated in fright at the sight of the flames. His mouth trembled and his skin looked clammy and ghostly white.

We don't have time for this. Argo tucked his bow into the strap on his knapsack and reached one hand under the boy's knees, the other below his back and under his armpit. He yelled in exertion as he lifted the boy up, first raising him to stand on one knee, then standing fully. He staggered once he took full height. Argo looked into his eyes, which hadn't moved from the flames. They were completely glazed over, and in their reflection, he saw a wall of fire behind him. Its heat grew and was rapidly engulfing them.

Something caught Argo's eye where the boy had initially fallen. There, in the dirt patch, lay the wooden arrowhead he'd carved for his mother long ago. He recognized it immediately and knew it was his. The wall of fire quickly encroached on it.

Argo looked at the boy and again at the fire, whose heat was now becoming too much to bear. Finally, he turned away from it and supported the boy once again and helped him as they ran back toward the hollow they'd come from. Wander knew where they were heading, and they all ran through together.

At once, they were back on the great plain.

CHAPTER 25

The Plain

Both Argo and the young boy's teeth were chattering from the icy wind. He set him down outside the hollow with his back against the tree, but the dead trunk provided little protection from the wind.

"Hey." He patted the young boy lightly on the cheek. "Are you all right?"

The boy said nothing and stared blankly past him.

Wander came up and smelled him, then licked him repeatedly on his face.

Finally the boy winced at this and snapped out of his confusion. He was young and dirty and smelled of terrible body odor and ash. He looked at Argo and slowly moved his mouth to signal something. He couldn't have been older than thirteen.

"It's okay," Argo said. "You're out of the fire. We're safe now." He dug through his pack and pulled out a waterskin and held it out for him, but the boy didn't take it, so Argo tilted it and slowly poured it into the boy's mouth. Most of it fell out and spilled on his brown pants, but then he started to slowly drink it and come back to his senses enough to grab the waterskin and drink on his own.

"Hey." Argo placed his hand on the boy's shoulder and shook it a little. "We need to get off this plain or we're going to freeze. Which hollow do we need to go in?" He looked around and saw a few trees scattered in the distance amongst the plain, including the one they'd first traveled through.

The boy gave him a confused look, then gradually shook his head. He opened his eyes wide and blinked a couple of times, then rubbed them awake. "That one." He feebly raised his hand and pointed to another dead and leafless tree away from the giant crevasse.

Argo turned and looked at Wander, who stared at the boy, her tail tucked between her legs. She licked him again. "We need to stand up and walk that way." He put on his knapsack and helped the boy to his feet. The child was visibly cold and crossed his arms over his chest. His skin was still white and clammy, though it seemed to be better than it was in the fire.

The sky was still clear and completely empty, and though the wind was a bitter cold, the sun high above the trio rested in the middle of the sky and provided some warmth as they traveled.

"That arrowhead you had. The wooden one. Where'd you get it?" Argo finally asked after moments of them walking together.

The boy didn't look up, only stared silently at the ground in front of them with his arms still folded. His bare feet were dirty and calloused all over and must have been freezing on the cold, hard ground.

"You call yourself *the Tree Traveler*, right?" Argo asked him.

The boy nodded his head, then he finally answered in a soft voice, "Yeah."

"Where'd you get that arrowhead?" Argo repeated.

The boy raised his head and looked off at the hollow in front of him. "A woman," he answered quietly. "She gave it to me."

"Tell me about her," Argo demanded.

The boy looked at his feet. "I don't remember. She was older and had brown hair, and I don't know. I never got too close. She was with The Rider."

"Go on. Keep going."

"She saw me hiding in the forest. I didn't want The Rider to see me. He was about to, then she distracted him. She knew I was afraid, and she left that for me."

"Then what happened?"

The boy kicked at a small rock. "Then they left."

Argo let out a long sigh, then wiped his hand across his face. "That woman was my mother," he finally said. "I made that arrowhead for her a long time ago."

The boy looked strangely up at him. "I'm sorry. I didn't mean to take it."

"No, don't feel bad," Argo told him, smiling at the thought of his mother. "She must've wanted you to have it."

The boy kept his eyes on the ground as they walked, making no reply.

"You've been here a while then?" Argo asked.

"I have."

Argo didn't say anything back. He wanted the boy to keep talking, so he stayed silent.

"I was with The Rider, and we were walking in the forest, and he told me to rest, and I didn't wanna rest, and I was scared, and I ran."

Argo nodded to the boy's story, trying to make him feel comfortable. "And you hid in a tree, didn't you?" he asked.

The boy nodded.

"That's how you found out how to move between the trees," Argo said, mostly to himself. "The Rider didn't come after you?" he asked.

"No." He shook his head and looked terrified again.

He's been moving between the trees, hiding from The Rider. He thinks he's going to find him one day... Which he may. "What's your name?" Argo asked.

The boy thought for a moment. Argo saw a confused look on his face, as if he hadn't remembered. "Gaius," he finally recalled.

"Gaius..." Argo repeated. "And you call yourself *the Tree Traveler.*"

The boy nodded. "I didn't want The Rider to find me."

"Well, Gaius, I'm supposed to go with The Rider too. That's why I'm here—to find him."

Gaius shuddered and looked up at Argo. "You're not going to take me to him? Are you?"

"No, no. You're safe. We're going back to the forest and then I'll leave you alone," Argo reassured the boy. "But we need to get back to exactly where we were when you took my torch."

"You promise you won't take me to him?" the young boy asked.

"I promise."

After a long stretch of the plain, they finally reached the hollow. Gaius entered through it first, and Argo and Wander followed closely behind him so he wouldn't run off. They walked back into a normal forest. Gaius led them to another nearby tree and went in that hollow, then another, and several more. Before long, they were back at the root cave. The rain had significantly lightened, and now it fell in a light mist. They stopped right outside it.

"Why'd you take my torch?" Argo asked him once they were back. "I'm not mad, it just doesn't seem like something someone would do if they were afraid."

The boy kept his eyes on the ground as he answered. "I dunno. I thought if I took it, you'd leave."

Argo almost rolled his eyes at the answer.

"I saw you and your dog near the village the other night" the boy continued. "The village looked mad, and The Rider was with someone else, I thought you were coming to get me. I thought you saw me so I ran."

Argo bent down "I saw your eyes, but I was scared too" he admitted. "That's why I drew my sword."

Argo looked down at him and felt sorry for him. "We're not here for you and I don't think the village knows you're doing this. Here. I have a little bit of food we can share, and then Wander and I have to go."

The three of them sat down beside the root cave and had some of the meat, cheese, and bread that Argo had packed. The boy laughed as Wander ate hers in a single bite, and she licked his face as he did so too.

The rain stopped completely, and the forest had returned to its natural state. Argo wanted to do more for the kid but knew he couldn't. *What am I supposed to do? I can't take him with me. He's too terrified and it only puts him in danger. I can't take him back to the village, I don't even know the way. If I leave him, at least he can continue living the way he has been. It seems like it's working out for him.*

Argo wrestled with the idea in his mind while watching Gaius eat. "Listen," he told him as they put away the meal and packed up. "I know it's scary. Look at Wander and I. We're both scared too. Everyone feels that way at some point.

Wander and I can't stay too much longer because we have to go meet The Rider, but if we can do something we're afraid of, you can too."

The young boy nodded and finished chewing his food while looking down at the ground again. Argo put his hand on his shoulder, then without finding the right words, took it off.

They said their goodbyes and watched as the boy slipped away across the stream and back into his hollow. A cold feeling of helplessness overcame Argo as knew that one day even The Tree Traveler would meet his fate.

"I'll come back for you, kid," he said under his breath.

CHAPTER 26

The Mouth

Argo continued down the trail, feeling regretful about the young boy's predicament. It pained him that there was nothing he could do for him but they were running out of time.

The river had now died down, and they followed a footpath to the side of it. Through the trees, he made out a large rock formation that swallowed up the horizon. As they drew closer, he could see that the river was flowing directly into the mouth of a large cave entrance.

Other than the terrifying tunnel from the previous day, he'd never seen a cave before, but he'd heard of them several times in stories told by the Lady of the Woods. In these tales, The Great Hero Adonillis would venture into a cave and need to navigate by torchlight. Then he'd find a great and evil monster dwelling inside that he would challenge and ultimately emerge victorious over. The thought of this made Argo sweat.

A raindrop fell innocently on his shoulder. Then more and more fell, and soon they were in the thick of a heavy rainfall once more. He threw his hood over his damp hair and pressed on. The rock formation grew larger and larger, and before long they were standing at the foot of a fantastic cave entrance large enough to fit his home multiple times over without touching a single wall. High as it stood, it still dwarfed in comparison to the massive trees towering over the rocks, swallowing them beneath their extraordinary covering. The mystery of the cavern seemed to carry in the breeze and evoked a dread of untamed natural wonder in its wake.

The river now gushed and flowed down the right side of the cave entrance. Its waters echoed through the hollowed chamber and reverberated loudly against the rock walls and out the entrance. The washed-out footpath they were standing on continued alongside the powerful river and faded away softly into the pitch-black darkness.

Argo and Wander stared cautiously but in awe at the grand entrance. Their eyes traced the outline and examined every nook and cranny. Bright green moss rose from the sides of the rock and crept up its uneven face. Like the valley, long vines flowed down and strung themselves out over the entrance. A heavy and humid air came flowing out of the mouth of the cave and smelled of wet rock and mildewy moss.

A roar of thunder echoed in the distance, and the rain began falling in sheets through the canopy. "We need to get inside, girl!" he called out to Wander, who whimpered at the thunder. Argo moved cautiously toward the mouth and was careful to not trip as the forest floor blended into the rock floor of the cavern. Once they were under its cover, he brought out his torch and struck it until its humble flame rose. It whirled around and calmed, then faintly bellowed toward the darkness. Argo and Wander looked each other in the eyes, then pressed on.

CHAPTER 27

The Cave

The light of the entrance dwindled quietly behind them, leaving Argo and Wander swallowed by the jet-black emptiness of the cave. The torch gave off a small sanctuary of light which they both held to dearly. They walked on a slight incline downhill, and Argo knew they had to be underground by this point. The river still raged beside them, though it was too dark to see past the torchlight. The sound of the running water provided a strange ambience and white noise, which seemed to almost come and go as they got used to it. The only points of solace that told him they were on the right path was that he could hear the water rushing beside him, and when he looked closely enough, he could see a lightened, well-trotted trail in the stone beneath them.

He felt Wander's scruffy fur tight against his leg as they walked. Her tail no longer wagged but was instead tucked between her legs and nearly swept the cold stone floor with each step. Though he could not see much, he now made out to his right the rocky ledge of the river. To his left, he saw nothing but the barren floor passing endlessly into the darkness. The light carried into this nothingness and grew fainter until it bled into the dark and became one with the cave. Still, they pressed on, step after quiet step, careful not to lose their footing.

Wander trotted to the river's edge and leaned in toward the water. Argo quickly pulled her back and scolded her. One false step and she would be lost to the ruthless abyss of the current.

Argo felt as if they were walking through a vast and empty void, perhaps through the night sky or under a deep lake. A powerful nothingness filled the air as dense as the river itself, soaking into every pore of his being. Argo's heart beat like a drum so loud that it could almost echo through the cave. He opened his eyes so wide they began to dry and pain him. His only touch was the ground beneath his feet and Wander's tense body pressed against his leg.

The smell of musty, wet stone loomed in the shadows and chilled his skin. He pulled his cloak over him with his free hand. The sound of the rushing water was now almost melodic and filled the cavern so loudly that it masked any other present sounds. He was forced to rely on his other senses, which were dulled to the point of hopelessness. The path continued down, deeper into the inner workings of the massive cave system. Wander stayed pinned at his side and had since stopped her whimpering.

The torchlight eventually fell on a crudely-carved passageway in the wall in front of them. Through this door ran the footpath they were on. Beside it, the river seemed to dip and run beneath the rock. Argo ran his torch over the passageway, carefully examining it for any clues that could help them. Above it, letters and symbols were carved primitively into the stone, the same text from the abandoned village before and on his torch. Argo looked at Wander, afraid to speak and break the facade of silence.

The two walked slowly through the doorway, which proved to be more of a tunnel than a door. The passage immediately turned left and then continued through a passage for a few steps before turning right. Through his light, he made out a fluorescent blue hue shining through the end of the tunnel. He placed his open hand on the back of Wander's neck and peered around the corner. The sight amazed him. In front of him lay another enormous chamber of the cavern, illuminated magnificently by a beautiful grove of trees, though instead of normal leaves, these trees had blue, fluorescent leaves that glowed flawlessly against the darkness. The trees were organized perfectly in rows and extended delightfully down the sides of the footpath. "Blue Hue," he said aloud to Wander, thinking back to the flower the Lady had shown him.

Beside them, the river ran gently and reflected the radiance of the glowing light against the far wall of the cavern. The light danced in rhythm against the rock in a fascinating spectacle. Above them, the ceiling of the cavern was illuminated with a map of the stars. Each star glowed amazingly with a blue sparkle that combined with the multitude of other stars, creating an ethereal palette of the night sky. In a far corner of the ceiling, a blue circle resembling the sun shined brightly against the stars. Not far from it, another smaller, blue semi-circle had been painted. Streaks of blue light flashed instantly across the background like shooting stars, in and out of existence within a moment. Wander looked upon the sight as well. Her tail wagged slightly, still nervous about where they were.

They walked cautiously down the traveled path that ran through the grove of trees. The orange glow of the torch meshed with the blueish white in an array of bright contrast. The flame bellowed softly down the path in the direction they were heading. Argo felt confident enough by the light supplied by the cavern that he extinguished the flame to conserve the fuel. After all, he had no idea how long they'd be in this darkness.

However, before doing so, he didn't want to put out his fire only to realize that the fluorescents were dependent on it somehow. He turned away from some of the trees and hid the torchlight with his cloak. The fluorescent light still shined dutifully, unaffected by the absence of firelight. Now he had the confidence needed and extinguished the flame. Thankfully, the blue light shone even brighter than before.

The fluorescent trees of blue were smaller than the ones in the forest and their canopies intertwined with one another across their three rows and made an ornate web of light between them bright enough to light up the cavern. They smelled of the same assortment of sweet and mysterious fragrances as the flowers from the Lady's garden. The ground was no longer the hard, cavernous rock they'd been walking on in the cave and instead was a soft layer of dark soil whose richness could be felt in every step. There were no rocks, nor grass, nor flowers, nor roots, as if someone had maintained it perfectly, though the path had been well traveled.

Argo bent down and looked closely at it, then picked up some of the dirt and ran it through his fingers.

There are horse tracks here.

He took another step forward and ran his hand across the dirt again.

Human tracks too. A lot of them. He studied the tracks even closer in the blue light. *The only tracks going back to the entrance are the horse tracks. All the human steps are going down the path... Has Emeric passed through yet?*

Wander scurried around the grove, taking in all the smells she could. She jutted from one tree to the next, running her nose across the soil with every step. Every so often as they walked, she'd come back to her master to check on him, then she'd go off again. Her paw prints outlined her trail in and out of the trees.

The caverns strange glow wrapped them comfortably, like a warm blanket, and Argo wondered if his mother had seen this ethereal beauty on her journey and felt the same way. Then he thought of his other friends and of his dad, who would never believe this sight.

A realization dawned on him. It had been a true shame that so many had lived such long lives and never seen a sight so magnificent as this. The path here was long and treacherous, but the reward of such beauty was worth it. It was difficult to not be upset at everybody for being so content in their daily lives. He considered himself lucky to have at least heard of such places from the Lady of the Woods. Neither his kin nor the village folk had any notion that such places existed, much less in tales. When Argo had listened to the stories, he'd close his eyes and imagine himself in these far-off lands, witnessing the sights firsthand. When he'd awake from these dreams, he found the world to feel subdued, gray, dull, and lifeless. Nothing could compare to seeing them in person like this. He saw their viewpoint, however, as much as he disagreed with it. There'd always been comfort in an easy life, part of which lay in the idea that it was so temporary. He'd thought about this several times while watching the Lady tend her garden, wondering what the point was in investing time and energy into something if the world was so transient and impermanent, and why a person should grow deep roots when death would uproot them. The smoothest tonic for it all was knowing that none of it mattered, and at times, Argo felt like everyone in his world understood that except for him. If none of it mattered, he wanted so desperately to ask his friends why they were even alive. He knew there must be some purpose to life other than waiting for the next, and what if they were already in a "next" life? What if they were stuck in some cycle that just repeats in perpetuity?

If there were one truth that prevailed, it was the truth that Argo had been infected and cursed with a terrible contagion of an idea that flowed through his veins and bled into his thoughts, transforming his way of living with its treacherous grasps. The full weight of the whole scenario saddened him. Part of him felt like he was cheating the experience of this path he was on. He felt as though he'd jumped the line and seen something he wasn't yet meant to see yet. The performers weren't ready, and the show was closed.

What's this like for those traveling with The Rider? Does he speak or provide context to the experience? Maybe he was like Wander, somehow perfectly in the exact intended place at the exact intended time. Perhaps his own free will and the forces of fate had collaborated carefully to create this moment precisely as intended. He looked at Wander, who wagged her tail cheerfully.

They hadn't quite reached it but could see ahead that the trail came to an end at the mouth of a large body of water fed by the river. The path led seamlessly to a small dock that extended into the water. It looked big enough for only a single boat to be docked on each side. Wander sprinted ahead to it, furiously sniffing at the ground. She locked onto another scent again.

"Wait, girl!" he called out after her.

She stopped and looked at him. He lightly jogged up to her and held her. With his hand on her back, she picked up the scent again and tracked it down near the base of the dock.

Another piece of cheese.

CHAPTER 28

The Ferryman

Argo watched as Wander lapped up the cheese in one big gulp. The pier was empty and made of old, rough wood that split and splintered at its seams. The rusty nails that held it together had shifted over time and now stuck out in places near the pier's ends. The wood smelled of subdued richness while the lake smelled fresh and clean. Two thick wooden poles stood higher than the rest at the end of the dock, as if it was the place to tie a vessel to. The water was as calm and smooth as glass, reflecting the starry night ceiling fantastically, and as dark as The Rider himself.

The dock was completely empty, except for a small wooden sign posted at the end.

Wait Here

The sign also had several other languages transcribed below it, none of which Argo could read, but their meanings seemed familiar. Strapped to one of the wooden poles next to the sign was a metal bracket meant to hold a torch.

Argo felt the old metal. Its orange rust rubbed off on his hands, the bracket nearly rusted through at points. Then he reached into his pack, pulled out his torch, and lit it. The flames whipped and danced and then came to rest, softly drifting out over the mysterious body of water. He gave the mount a good shake to make sure it wouldn't fall, then carefully placed his torch in it. It fit perfectly.

He allowed the flame to burn for several moments as he peered out over the water, which carried endlessly into the vast expanse of darkness. Feeling that the flame was unwanted in the already lit cave, he extinguished it and placed it back in his knapsack. Behind him, he heard Wander at the edge of the stone shoreline drinking some of the water. She finished and trotted merrily over to Argo.

The two sat down between the rusty nails at the edge of the wooden decking and peered at the unique horizon over the water. He fell deep into thought about the possibilities of what lay next for them. Moments passed, and finally he lay back, his head on his pack, and gazed up at the illuminated stars. His eyes searched deep into the faux night sky illuminated on the ceiling above him. The stars magically moved and stirred gracefully, and he followed them across the sky. Every so often, streaks of shooting stars cut across the map in long, blueish-white stretches.

Wander fell fast asleep, her head resting on his chest. She snored lightly with each breath, and her tongue poked slightly out of her mouth. He petted her head gently, dragging his fingers behind her ear and down her neck until he, too, fell into slumber.

A swift kick to the side woke him up. Argo jumped awake and scurried backward. Wander snapped awake as well and barked and growled wildly, backing up with her master. Argo sloppily reached for his sword and drew it from its sheath, holding it outward toward the foe standing over him. "Who are you?" Argo bellowed. Wander barked and growled the same.

The man stood over them without a word. He was tall and slender, and he wore a large-brimmed hat that cast a moonlit shadow over his face. In this shadow, he held a long pipe, smoke gently rising from it. He dressed plainly in long pants and a white, long-sleeve blouse, sleeves rolled up. Instead of a cloak, an intricately designed brown blanket was draped over his body with a clean-cut hole in the center for his head. A strong scent of smokey-yet-mysterious tobacco lingered on him.

Argo lay on the deck, holding his sword out toward him while he scanned him from head to toe, upset at himself for allowing someone to get the jump on him and Wander.

The man looked down at Argo, completely unphased by the sword inches from his chest. The man was unarmed except for a small knife at his waistband that had to have served as a tool more so than a weapon. He couldn't have been The Rider either, for he seemed much too normal and of average height. His unusual casualness in the encounter seemed off-putting and made Argo feel even more confused, though he sensed no threat from him. The man calmly grabbed his pipe out of his mouth, then turned and spat over the deck and into the water. "Who're you?" he said in a deep and raspy voice.

Wander seemed on guard, though not aggressive, and watched cautiously from behind her master.

"I'm Argo. This is Wander," he answered, still holding his sword to the man's chest.

The man put his pipe back in his mouth. Smoke billowed smoothly out of the shadow. He remained completely unphased by his visitors. "I'm the ferryman. This here is the ferry," he said as he turned slightly to the wooden boat tied to the dock.

Argo leaned over to look behind the figure and thought for a moment. "Then we're here to take the ferry," he replied.

The man stoked his pipe. The smoke was white and contrasted strongly with his shadowy figure. He reached out and with two fingers brushed the sword aside.

Argo lowered the blade.

"Ferry's not for you, kid," he said calmly, then turned and walked away to the land.

Argo looked surprised at Wander then called back "Why not?"

"You're alive," he said without breaking stride or looking back.

Argo stumbled to his feet and quickly gathered his belongings. Then he ran to catch up with the ferryman. Wander trotted behind him.

"I'm going to find The Rider," he said once he caught up. "I have a letter." He fumbled through his pockets and held out the letter.

The man didn't look back, only kept walking as if they weren't there.

"Is The Rider that way? Over the water?" Argo asked him. "Please, I'm running out of time."

The man said nothing. His pace was slow yet confident, and he walked without a single sound, almost as if he were weightless. Strangely, his boots left no imprints in the soft dirt.

After everything he'd experienced on the journey so far, being ignored built a frustration in Argo. "I apologize for pestering you. It's just too important that we continue on our path." He gave the man a moment to respond.

He didn't. Instead, he approached one of the trees and carefully sorted through the fluorescent leaves, plucking a few at a time. His hands looked rough in the light.

Argo watched him impatiently. He folded his arms across his chest like his father had always done. "If you won't take us, is there another route?"

The man ignored him and continued to pick the leaves. He reached under his poncho and pulled out an old cloth bag folded through his belt and put the leaves in it. The bag glowed a dim blueish white through the thin material.

In the light of the leaves, Argo could make out the man's face. He looked to be a good number of years older than himself, though not quite as old as his father, and he had a scruff and grizzled look about him. The leaf-light reflected perfectly off his pitch-black eyes, which were honed sharply in on finding the best leaves. He held them in his rough hand and ran his fingers over each of them, inspecting them closely. Then he moved to another area of the tree, pulled some in to smell them, and picked the ones he thought were good.

Wander laid down in the dirt and kept her eyes glued to the man, curiously watching as he worked.

He picked one after another until he filled the bag. Once it was plump, he twisted the top and placed it back through his belt. Then without a word, he turned and walked back to the dock, straight past the two as if they weren't there.

They followed anxiously behind him. The walk back to the dock was silent. Smoke from the strange man's pipe floated like a chimney and then promptly sank down and rested in a thin layer above the dirt. It smelled sweet and flavorful, like something familiar yet entirely foreign, and the scent reminded Argo of his father sitting in front of the hearth or on the patio, puffing away at his pipe. Argo had never picked up the habit himself but occasionally smoked it with his friends. Now the smoke seemed inviting in a way it never had before.

As they made their way, he saw that a rope fastened in several loops was tied to the man's belt as well, and with each step, the coil swayed and bounced against his leg, all remaining silent as the cave itself. The three of them made it back to the pier without another word.

The man took his seat peacefully on one of the pillars at the end of the dock and stared out to sea, puffing his pipe in long, drawn breaths. The smoke drifted easily over the water. Instead of dissipating, it slowly floated down to the surface and drifted out into the darkness like leaves on the water.

Argo set his pack down and leaned up against the other pillar beside the man. He stared out over the sea as well and contemplated the nature of his predicament. Wander walked casually over to the strange man and sat next to him. He turned to her, then lifted his arm and petted her gently, stopping behind her ears to scratch them tenderly. She closed her eyes and embraced it. Argo watched the two and wasn't sure how to take it. He studied the man suspiciously from a distance. Although he faced away, he sensed a longing in the man's presence. He'd seen the look before—the same look his father held when he sat for long hours on the front porch and stared off profoundly into the Woods. An unmistakable un-wholeness.

Argo thought back to his conversations with the Lady. From what she'd told him, a man, although whole in himself, could easily become half a man if the right components were removed from his life. In each love, a man gave a piece of himself away, sometimes more though oftentimes less. And sometimes, that piece was destroyed or even returned damaged, never to fit as perfectly as it did before. Argo had seen the ruins of a once-beautiful creation severed from its roots in his father's loss of his mother. It had always been a great irony that something that brought so much joy could bring so much pain.

Argo finally built up the courage to speak again. "You don't have to answer. I know that by all rights, I'm not even supposed to be here. I received a letter from The Rider several days ago. My days are wearing thin. I came into the forest on my own. Wander chose to travel with me. I know not the path, but I'm finding the way… or so I believe. I'm seeking out The Rider. I made it this far, and I need to cross if this is indeed the right way. I understand if you won't take me. Either way, I'm not going to stop. I'll either find a way or I'll make one."

The man remained motionless, one hand still calmly petting Wander, and the other holding his pipe in place.

Argo waited patiently, but he got no response. Finally, he shook his head hopelessly and dug through his pack. He pulled out his torch, then struck at his flintstone until a flame spiraled upward and shone its light on the dock.

The man stopped petting Wander and turned around suddenly. His pitch-black eyes focused on the flame, and Argo could see them clearly now in the light. "That torch." The man stood and moved quickly to Argo. "Where'd you get it?" He reached for the torch.

Argo put up no fight and let the man have it.

He glared deep into the flame and then inspected the inscription on the shaft.

"My friend gave it to me," Argo answered, unsure of what the man wanted to hear.

"Who? Who gave it to you?" he demanded, still in a cool and calm tone.

"The Lady of the Woods," Argo answered.

The man's illusion of cool mysticism was shattered. His black eyes sank in bewilderment, and he immediately looked human in a way that he'd hidden before. He quickly turned away and looked over the water, hiding his expression.

Argo and Wander both looked at one another in confusion.

"This Lady. Tell me about her." The man stepped closer to the edge of the dock and looked out over the water.

The man's sudden interest took Argo aback. "Well, she's the light of the forest. She's lovely. Radiant even. One of my dearest friends. She helped inspire me to undertake this journey. I went to her before I came into the Woods, and she gave me this torch. Said that it was given to her by someone she used to know and that it would help us."

The man remained silent. He crossed his arms across his chest and puffed away once again at his pipe. The smoke rose over his hat and sank once more over the water. "Someone that she used to know," the man repeated to himself. "That right?" More smoke blew out, choppy and uneasy.

"She said the flame blows toward death," Argo continued.

"Now it points out over the water," the man answered solemnly.

"I suppose it points to where I need to go," Argo responded.

The man stood overlooking the water. He said nothing in return.

"Do you know her? The Lady?" Argo asked.

"I do." He answered. "Did." He turned over his shoulder and nodded to the boat. "Go on, now. Get in."

CHAPTER 29

The Ferry

The vessel had been made from the same old, decaying wood as the pier, though it somehow held perfectly watertight. It could easily hold eight men comfortably and had a flat, wood-plank decking that Argo presumed held The Rider's horse. A small platform was built into the stern with a long pole extending from it, which Argo assumed was where the ferryman stood as he piloted the craft.

Argo boarded with one foot after the other. The boat shifted under his weight, and a wave of ripples echoed across the water. Wander jumped in after him and slid across the decking on her nails. Her legs wobbled awkwardly and then spread out when she landed. Once she stopped sliding, she slowly stood up and struggled to keep her balance.

The boat rocked with the motion of the two of them, then came to rest steadily on the surface, the ripples once again traveling over the mirrored surface before quickly returning to its calm and glasslike state. Argo took off his knapsack and strapped it to the decking below his seat with rope that had been attached to the deck. He tightened the seat down and gave it a good shake to make sure it was secured.

The ferryman, still holding the torch, stepped calmly in after them, and the boat remained completely motionless as he boarded. He maneuvered to the pointed bow and placed the torch in another bracket. It fit snugly, and the ferryman twisted it down into place. Then in a single, unbroken motion, he glided gracefully between his passengers to his spot at the stern. He leaned down and grabbed the lashing line tied to the dock, and in another smooth and quick gesture, he powerfully flicked his wrist. The rope whipped in his hands and uncoiled from the dock, tossed in the air, and fell magnificently into a perfectly wrapped coil in the boat. The boat gently floated away from the dock as he did so. Then he picked up the coil and tucked it beneath his platform. Next, he grabbed the tall steering pole and gave a gentle push from the dock. The boat rocked back and forth softly and floated out from the deck.

The ferryman gave a gentle push of his pole, and the magnificent grove gradually faded in the distance. The boat glided across the water beautifully and gave the feeling of floating through space. A small wake pushed away from it and out across the surface, rippling the reflection of the stars and moon above. The orange glow of torchlight beat bravely against the cool, damp air.

Argo felt overwhelmed with the wonderment of being terrified in awe, as a traveler would feel, rowing across the ether of the stars. "Why the change of heart?" Argo asked. "You knew The Lady?"

The man stayed quiet for a moment. He looked over his passengers and looked intent on piloting the craft. Finally, he took a breath and answered, "Didn't just know The Lady." He stopped there. "I loved her."

Argo didn't know how to respond. A thousand questions raced through his mind, though he only asked one. "And she loved you?"

"She did," the ferryman replied. His gaze stayed locked to the open water in front of them.

Only the strange glowing sky and the torch lit their vessel now. The lake was still as glass in all directions, except for in their wake, and the mirroring surface magnificently reflected the fluorescent stars above. Wander had regained her confidence and stood on her hind legs, looking curiously over the side of the boat. She watched the water push aside from the boat and ripple away. It moved like a thick oil rather than water, yet it made no noise when it beat against the wooden body of the vessel.

Argo looked strangely at the man. "You were alive then? And recently?" he asked, not sure where to begin.

"I was, kid. Not recent though. The Lady's more than you think." He gave another long push with his pole and puffed at his pipe. "It was long ago. Before your time." He took another momentary pause, then continued. "She ain't of that place. The world you and I are from. The one with your village. She's somethin' more."

"What do you mean?" Argo asked, scooting closer to the edge of his seat.

"What I mean is, she's somethin' more," he repeated. "She was alive when I was alive, and I'm assumin' she was alive while you were too."

Argo caught what the ferryman was saying. "I understand," he answered.

He gave another long stroke with his pole. "We were happy together. Then one day I got my letter, same as you. That was new at that time. And I didn't want to leave her. So, I didn't." He finally looked away to the side of the boat. "Next thing I knew, The Rider rode me down. Caught me right there at our home."

"So, you're here as punishment?" Argo asked.

"It's all punishment, kid," he answered.

"What is?"

"Bein' without her," he answered.

Argo said nothing in return, just nodded and tried his best to understand.

"I was different though. The Lady and I made a deal with The Rider. She did the talkin'. He wasn't going to listen to me. In the end, I went with him and ended up stayin' in the Woods. Just waitin' for her to one day travel herself. Those days turned to years. Hell, I waited so long, the memories of her began to fade. Lost to the Woods like everythin' else." He sighed and let out another long plume of smoke. The brim of his hat sat low and covered his face as he spoke. "Before long, all that remained were the memories of how I felt when I was with her. Even then, I waited. Few others joined me, all for reasons of their own." He paused again. "Memories, kid… worse than any wound."

Argo felt the pain in the man's voice. His words rippled through the air like the waves on the water, falling still once again on his smooth appearance. Argo thought back to the carving of the Lady in the stone structure. "You stayed in the stone houses? In the Woods?" he asked the ferryman.

"I did," he calmly responded.

"I saw your carving then. Of the Lady," he told him, assuming he'd been the one responsible for it.

"That was me, all right," he answered back. "You see, a man's heart can only bear a weight for so long. And I reached my breaking point and had enough. Made my way here and struck another deal with The Rider, this time on my own. Told him I would ferry him and travelers until I saw her once more. I needed a change and wanted to be here to guide her when her time was finally called. Only then can I allow myself to pass on to the next life." He pushed the pole again, this time with more power than the others. "Though, I worry I won't even recognize her after all this time. Or she won't recognize me."

As Argo listened, he noticed how the man's pain was sinking into his heart. There was something unique about feeling someone else's suffering. It spread to those near it like an illness, infecting the hearts and minds of those in its wake. Then he looked out over the water once more and wondered how many others felt the same as this man. He wondered if his mother felt the same toward them.

If he could stay and wait, why couldn't she?

The man must have noticed the dreary expression fall over his passenger. "Kid," he said, "I chose this. I would do it all again if I could."

"You would do what all again? Be with her and go through all of this?" Argo asked.

The ferryman grunted and gave a slight nod. "Wouldn't change a thing."

"What about meeting her at the end of all this, you know, on the other side?" Argo asked.

"I could. That would be the easiest way," the ferryman answered.

"Then why don't you?"

He stoked the ember in his pipe once more and lowered it after a long inhale. "That's easy, kid. Makes sense even. But let me tell you something. Love ain't logical. True love, the kind to make a man wait eternally for, deserves more. Don't you understand? Waitin' for her at the end." He shook his head. "It's too easy. It's what everyone would have done and what she would be expectin'. But to stay? To wait all this time for her? That's givin' her somethin' special... And I want her to feel special."

The ferryman's words drifted off, and Argo had no words to reply. He was on his own quest, one much longer than his. Argo could see where the man was drawing his passion from, though he didn't fully relate to it. Moments passed until Argo spoke up once again. "When you were alive, so long ago, how was it?"

"What do you mean?"

"The Lady used to tell me tales when I would see her. Mostly about The Great Hero Adonillis. Tales of bravery, love, and passion. Was the world really like that? You said The Rider was new at that time, right?"

The man answered calmly. "The Great Hero Adonillis... Of course." The pipe's smoke drifted off the brim of his hat. "The world was like that. At a time. I saw it changin' as The Rider started guidin' people away. Can't imagine how it is now. Let me tell you something, kid. Bravery, love, passion... those will always exist. What fades is the will to act on them. No Rider will end that. That's between a man and himself." He paused for a moment. "I'm here because I want to be here. I want my love to burn like that torch there, against the void. To guide my Lady back to me."

Argo listened carefully to the man.

"I do it because of her," he answered. "She got me. Made me completely vulnerable. That's what love is in the end. A complete surrender ... Bravery comes in many forms, kid"

Argo reflected on the ferryman's words and thought of his father and all the time he spent living without his mother. He'd never considered what it took for him to stay all those years just waiting for his letter.

Then he thought of his own quest. "I'm torn," Argo finally said. "I'm trying so hard to be brave. That's really one of the reasons why I'm on this quest. I... well...," he began to stutter, "People don't talk like this back in the village. I just don't know if what I'm doing is foolish. I don't know what's right anymore."

The man rowed silently. "Are you afraid?"

"Very," Argo answered softly, certain his concern echoed in his voice.

"You want me to turn this vessel around?"

"No."

"That's bravery, kid," the ferryman responded.

Argo fell silent and nodded, then turned to look over the front of the boat, hiding his subtle smile.

CHAPTER 30

The Water

Argo and the ferryman continued speaking for a long while as he piloted the vessel through the darkness. They spoke about the Lady, and Argo filled the air with sweet memories that enticed the man as charmingly as any music. His mood lightened, and Argo could even make out a smile or two every so often through the torchlight, which burned honorably through the black.

The water beneath them began to flow more heavily, and the ferryman used the long pole to skillfully navigate around large boulders jetting out from the surface. The reflection of the stars and moon above disappeared in the swath of running water. Wander, who'd fallen asleep under Argo's seat, was now awake and trying her best to brace herself with the current. Suddenly they hit a small rapid and the boat plunged slightly between boulders as high as the ferryman's knees.

"Hold on to that dog of yours, kid. This part is rougher than usual."

The sound of rapids grew louder and louder, and they felt the pull of the boat beneath them. The ferryman dumped the ash from his pipe overboard and tucked the pipe into his waistband. Then he grabbed the long pole with both hands.

With the deck tumbling beneath them, Argo gripped his seat tightly with one hand and enveloped the other snugly around Wander, who had started to whimper in panic. Then he wrapped part of his leg around her to cage her underneath the seat.

The boat plunged again, even deeper than before, then hit the drop sharply and bounced against the bottom of the rapid. Argo's stomach lifted in his chest with the drop.

The ferryman stood immortally poised on the back, the same as he'd done for the whole boat ride. He navigated the rapids skillfully, pushing and pulling on the long pole with the tides. The boat settled again and stopped, then immediately rushed forward uncontrollably, tossing left, then tossing right.

Wander whined loudly from beneath the seat and kicked frantically, trying desperately to escape. Argo struggled to hold her, and the small boat rocked in the rapids, which were growing in size, their roars growing even louder. The boulders that towered out of the river beside them rose higher than the ferryman, blotting out the stars on the horizon. The water clashed cruelly against their great walls and shot around swiftly, even more vicious than before.

The boat slammed loudly against a rapid. Argo's grip slipped off his wooden bench and he slid down to the right of his seat before being thrown against the side of the boat. Wander slid with him and wailed even louder than before. Water splashed up against his face and soaked him entirely, and it's cold bite crawled down his spine and chilled him to his core. Numbness ran from his chest to his fingertips, and still he held on to Wander and the seat.

The boat calmed, then immediately jerked the other way. The two were tossed down the seat and forced up mightily against the other side.

"Hold on, kid!" the ferryman yelled over the wrath of the rapids. "Ain't ever been this bad!" He stood strongly at the back of the boat and still seemed unaffected by the chaos.

Argo looked fearfully up at him, then gave a small nod as the boat rocked once more in the opposite direction. He turned and looked off the bow of the vessel. Waves smashed against the torchlight as the flame thrashed in circles. It remained lit, though they could barely make out what they were heading into.

Suddenly, the light shone on a large body of white water leading off an endless drop into the darkness. The sound of rushing water was now unbearably loud, and it tore powerfully through the cavern. "Hold on!" the man shouted.

Over the bow, Argo watched the flame of the torch immediately shift directions and blow toward him. The boat plunged weightlessly, and Argo felt himself lift from the vessel, then thump violently back into the seat, then get thrown like a ragdoll up and over the seat until he tumbled to the front of the boat. He placed a death grip around a rope tied to the front and felt the front dip sharply.

Wander came tumbling toward him, still wailing in agony. He reached out to grab her, but just as his fingers felt her fur, the bow shot upward and launched Wander up and out the side of the vessel. "No!" Argo cried painfully as a wave of water crashed against his face.

She was gone.

He crawled to the side of the craft and threw his arms over the edge, holding himself in place. By a miracle, he saw her snout and paws rise from the water's surface amidst the rapids, lit only by the torch and stars above. He pulled himself higher on the side of the boat.

"Let her go! She's gone!" the man yelled over the crashing of the rapids.

Argo looked at him as terror crawled up his throat. He crawled across the bench and hurled himself overboard into the black sea. He hit the water terribly and was immediately consumed by the cold rush that dragged him under. He kicked and clawed forcefully in all directions and tumbled head over heels in the current. His lungs were on fire and his heart beat like a wild animal's.

Fear and panic and shock and pain raced through his veins, and his world was pitched black, filled with the dread of a cold, deadly abyss. He slammed against a rock wall, then was pulled under and pinned against it. He kicked and clawed and felt his leg against another wall. He pushed hard against it, knocking himself loose and back into the current once more. He shut his eyes and kept kicking as hard as he could, then gritted his teeth, tucking his chin close to his chest and placing his hands behind and over his head, and curled into a ball. The rushing tide took him once again and tossed him even farther downstream, forcing him back to the surface.

Once his head emerged, he took a long gasp of air. The rapids ruthlessly swallowed him down again into the freezing waters. He inhaled a mouthful of it.

He tried to cough it up while still pulled under and choked even more. The water shot him back to the surface. He instantly broke into a panic of coughing and gagging.

Wander slammed lifelessly against him.

He grabbed her, then wrapped his arm around her and grabbed his shirt with that hand, holding her locked in place. He struggled to keep her head above the surface. She felt like a ragdoll in his arms. He kicked aggressively and pushed against the current with his other hand. He only felt the will to survive.

The swift current dropped them down again and shot them back up to the surface, insistently throwing them around with the tide. He refused to lose her again and paddled ceaselessly with his free arm, which now burned from exhaustion. His feet felt powerless yet still he kicked with all of his being.

Just then, a rope fell over his free hand and tightened around it. He gripped it and held on for his life. It pulled him strongly against the current. His head dipped beneath the surface and rose again. The water rushing against it beat endlessly and pushed past him and Wander.

Finally, a hand reach down and gripped his forearm and lifted him powerfully out of the water. The two fell harshly against the decking of the boat.

Wander sprawled across the deck. Argo opened his eyes and coughed out the freezing water. Through the torchlight, the ferryman stood tall over them. He quickly coiled the rope from his belt loop and threw it aside. He bent down over Wander and pushed against her chest.

Argo immediately rolled over to them. His mind raced and couldn't comprehend what had happened. The boat still rocked from side to side, but the current had died down.

"Wander! No, no no no no," Argo repeated as he patted her face. His tears were flowing uncontrollably now, and panic rose from his gut and through his head.

The ferryman kept pushing.

"No no no, come on, Wander! Come on!" Argo cried.

The ferryman pushed even harder, trying desperately to force the water out of her.

Wander spat water across the deck. She opened her eyes faintly and tried to gag, though nothing came out. She could barely keep her eyes open.

Argo wrapped his arms tightly around her and cried uncontrollably, the tears becoming lost on his soaking face. He closed his eyes and felt both Wander's lungs expand and deflate in a labored way, still attempting to catch her breath. Her front paw was terribly crooked to the side. Cuts through large patches of her fur and along her head and back were bleeding light red.

The man stood and looked on at them, drying his hands on the blanket over his chest. Beneath the brim of his hat, he twitched a subtle sigh of relief. He walked quietly back to the long pole and gracefully maneuvered the vessel onto the smooth river once again.

CHAPTER 31

The Smoke

Argo and Wander lay sprawled out across the decking.

The ferryman stepped off his platform, removed his hat, then set it carefully down. He grabbed the blanket around him at the shoulders and lifted it off and over his head. He put his hat back on and covered the two with his blanket.

Wander breathed harshly, her lungs struggling with each breath. Argo wiped his tears away with his wet hand. His nostrils burned with the taste of cold water and his head swelled from the emotion. He rolled over and removed his knife from its sheath and cut a long, narrow strip off the end of his cold, wet cloak. He rolled closer to Wander and fixed her broken paw back in place. She watched wearily as she lay, then let out a loud cry when he adjusted it. She had no strength to put up a fight. Then she rolled over and rested her head on the decking and closed her eyes.

Argo held her paw in place, then wrapped the piece of his cloak around it. He wanted to hold her but decided it would be best to let her sleep comfortably. Instead, he sat back on the bench and dropped his head in his hands. The ferryman watched him without a word, as stoic as before.

Argo pulled off the ferryman's blanket and wrapped it around Wander. Then he gritted his teeth and untied his cloak. Each movement pained him, but he laid it out on the decking to air out as best as he could, then pressed the water out of his blouse and trousers. They were cold and suctioned against his clammy body.

Fortunately, the air in the cave felt comparatively warm and gave off a unique comfort.

"Water'll be easy now. Best get some rest," the man said calmly.

Argo sat back on the bench and hunched over his knees, then lay across the seat and rested his head against the grainy wood.

The boat traversed across the glossy surface, the dim torchlight's flame dancing prevalently against the shadows, beating like the heart of an animal. The sound of the rapids had faded softly behind them, and now only the soft sound of the vessel cutting through the water and the man's long pole maneuvering the boat carried through the cave.

***

The ferryman watched Argo from his position on the stern in admiration. He grabbed his pipe from below the platform and tucked it in his belt with the bowl protruding from the top. Never in his days had he seen such unquestionable recklessness and disregard for someone's own safety, yet he felt an eerie familiarity toward what he'd witnessed. He knew the love that filled Argo's heart because he had the same love for The Lady, who now sat a world away from him, away from this madness. He couldn't find the words to say that he'd been contemplating his own time and dedication to his sworn duty. Before, he'd felt at the end of his rope while waiting. Now, he was freshly rejuvenated by what he'd witnessed. He would've dived headfirst into this black hole of a river for The Lady had fate required such, yet his challenge demanded something else entirely. His was a slow burn, the degradation of time that slowly chips away at the strongest foundations, like a river slowly cutting into a valley. Seeing the young man's courage and compassion toward his companion filled the ferryman's heart like a quenched thirst after a drought. He whisked the long pole gracefully in the water, watching his passenger lie awake and stare longingly at the fire, and then at Wander, who lay in a deep sleep below him.

Argo's hand dangled off the bench and rested on Wander's fur. He stroked his fingers behind her ear to keep a connection between them and let her know that he was still there.

The ferryman pulled out the bag of fluorescent leaves, which shone dimly through the sack. Then he stepped down from his platform and sat on its edge, reached into his pocket, and pulled out thin leaf.

Argo turned and watched him as he crushed and tore the blue leaves apart in his fingertips and placed them delicately in the thin leaf, then rolled it tightly together. When he finished, he placed it on the bench and surgically conducted the procedure again, this time placing the new pieces into the bowl of his pipe. He packed each layer down carefully, one after the next. Holding the pipe upright in his hand, he walked to the front of the vessel and stepped effortlessly over Argo's bench to the torch at the bow, where he first lit the rolled leaf in the flame, then stoked it lightly in his mouth. The ember burned a fine blue. He held it out to Argo, who curiously sat up and received it.

"What is it?" he asked.

"Not sure. Stay down here long enough, you come to appreciate new things," the man answered. "Close enough to tobacco."

***

Argo put it to his lips and filled his mouth with a cool smoke. It instantly relaxed him and relieved the tension that had built up in his muscles. His weight sank into the seat. He released his breath slowly. The smoke rose and fell back to the rear of the boat as they traveled; then it traveled up the platform and fell over the side, as if it were wind through the mountains. He watched this, then closed his eyes, rubbing them gently. It tasted like tobacco he'd smoked before with his friends and father, except this had a light sweetness and a fine bitterness on the exhale. He did feel slightly better, if just for the moment.

The man leaned closer to the flame and breathed in the fire through his pipe. The torchlight illuminated his face and reflected off his pitch-black eyes. He stoked the tobacco-like fire, and the smoke rose and slid off the brim of his hat, which still sat low over his face. He finished and moved gracefully back to his position. Instead of sitting down, he lifted the wood he'd once stood on and pulled out an instrument from the compartment underneath. It had long strings extending from a hollow, wooden body. He sat down on the bench facing Argo and put his pipe back in his mouth, then plucked elegantly at the strings. A beautiful harmony resonated from it and filled the cavern. Together, they sat and listened to the music in deep appreciation as the boat carried them peacefully on.

Argo inhaled and listened in appreciation. His concern for Wander seemed to momentarily fade away, the music as soul stirring as any sunrise or sunset, reassuring them all that everything would be okay. Wander opened her eyes and watched the man for a moment, then closed them gently and fell back asleep.

He continued to naturally pluck away at the strings in an otherworldly way Argo had never seen or heard before. The song carried on and then fell into a melodic rhythm of him gently playing the same notes. "I admire what you did back there," he finally said while still playing.

"Thanks," Argo replied.

"As a man, I believe it's important to give credit where it's due," he reassured his passenger.

"That's good to hear for once. It means a lot to me," Argo answered, exhaling smoke as he spoke. "My friends would've called it reckless."

The man nodded. "I know. I met one. Just earlier."

"Emeric." Argo nodded.

"The fat one," the man added.

"That was him."

"Don't expect others to understand, kid," the ferryman replied, still playing his music. "Men like you and I can't expect everyone to understand. Not in 'em." He inhaled once again and slowly released it. "People only understand what's in their capacity to understand... If the journey feels right to you, then it's right to you. That's the simple nature of it."

"You're right," Argo agreed. "I guess I just want others to feel the same way sometimes."

"Wouldn't that be nice? Some people feel a need to pull you down to their level. Makes 'em feel better about their own failures. Helps to justify the life they're livin'."

The music still resonated beautifully through the distance between them. "You know,' said Argo, "when I jumped down to save my friend the other day—Emeric—I did it instinctively, out of some need to be a hero. When I jumped in for Wander, it was different. I was afraid. Not of what might happen to me, but of what might've happened to her. I surprised myself, if I'm being honest." He pulled another drag from the thin leaf. "But this time, I didn't mind dying in there. In the water. Some part of me was hoping that Wander would come out safely and I wouldn't. Part of me was hoping the water would just sweep me away out of this mess, never to see the end of my own tale. Just let it all end. Maybe I wouldn't have to endure this anymore." Defeated, Argo looked away.

"Listen, kid." The man looked up at Argo and met his eyes for the first time. They were as black as the night was dark. "The only true greatness is in being truly good. All else is vanity. Let it die."

As they neared the shoreline, Argo rearranged his pack for Wander to fit inside, while the ferryman packed his instrument away neatly and guided the vessel lovingly to the bank. It beached against the sandy shoreline of the river and drove up and over it, coming to an abrupt stop.

A glimmer of sunlight shone through an opening some distance away and lit the cavern magnificently. Wander snapped open her eyes and pulled her head up, then looked at her master tenderly. He had never left her side. Now that they were beached, he carefully lifted her hind legs and slid the pack beneath her, then pulled it up and over until only her head and paws were hanging out from the top. He lifted the pack and swung it around on his back, where it rested awkwardly yet kept her broken paw out of the way. Then he carefully climbed out and jumped to the sandy bank below, cautiously turning to not add any stress to Wander.

He walked a few steps, then turned back to the man. "I forgot to mention," Argo said as he remembered one last note. "There's a kid in the forest. About twelve years old who calls himself *The Tree Traveler*. His name's Gaius. I met him just outside the mouth of the cave. He's a good kid, just scared, and might need looking after. He was traveling with The Rider and ran away. Now he's hiding in the Hallowed Woods. I wish I could've done more to help him."

The man gave a slight smile and nodded. "I'll look into it."

Argo gave a small nod in return and walked away.

"Kid, the torch." The man gestured to it at the front of the vessel.

Argo looked at it for a moment. "Is that the end of the cave?" he asked, referring to the light ahead.

"That is," the man answered.

Argo thought for a moment. "You better keep it. I'm sure The Lady will appreciate it."

The man nodded once again in return. "Kid," he said once more.

Argo turned to him.

"We're only just men. What more can man do than fight against his tide?" With that, the ferryman pushed off the bank and drifted gracefully back into the river.

Argo watched the flame of the lantern desperately pull toward him as it dissipated in the distance.

Book Three

CHAPTER 32

The Day

Argo and Wander emerged from a small opening in the side of a shady hill and back into the Hallowed Woods which they had grown accustomed to. It smelled fresh and clean compared to the air in the cave. Scents of oaky moss carried in the cool springtime wind and beat gently against his now-dry clothes.

In front of the exit, a beaten footpath led down the hill and into the tall trees. Instead of moss and overgrown roots, the forest floor was smooth with luscious green grass, which flowed and ebbed with the breeze. Songbirds and other critters played their tunes in the distance, filling the forest with life.

Argo walked down the path to a nearby tree and carefully lay Wander down against it. He took a seat next to her and rested with his back against the bark, petting her behind her ears. She tenderly gave in to the touch, slowly licking toward Argo's hand but only getting her own nose. He gave a soft smile, then gave her a gentle kiss on the forehead and nuzzled it playfully. It pained him to see her in such a state.

He carefully pulled the cloth knapsack closer and reached behind her, grabbing the remaining food to split between them. Their appetites had ceased in the cave and were now back with a vengeance. He tried to eat his share slowly so he could savor each bite, but soon realized that he wasn't hungry after all. The nerves of his last day were too much for him to think about food. Instead of finishing his share, he tore off bits of the meat, cheese, and bread and pressed them together to feed Wander, who mustered up as much energy as she could to lift her head and take it in. She cleaned every last crumb.

When finished, Argo rested his head against the rough tree and closed his eyes. They fell like heavy curtains, but a single thought kept him awake. He reached into his breast pocket and pulled out the letter from The Rider. The parchment was torn at the seams, crumbled, stained with blood, and soaked through and stuck to itself. It nearly fell apart in his hand. He delicately unfolded each edge and read it once more:

ARGO

TONIGHT

This time felt different than all the others. There was no number, only the immensity of a single word.

If he had stayed home like everyone else, he would have been eating his final meal in the comfort of his warm home with his father and friends, planning to meet The Rider that night. But he hadn't stayed home. Instead, he was days away, lost deep in a strange and foreign land. A strange guilt overcame him, like missing an appointment with a friend. He also felt surprised about how much time had passed in the cave. They must've been down there for a while, but to think that it was a whole day didn't seem quite right to him. He looked up at the sky and could tell it was sometime in the morning, though the high trees hid the sun. The smell of rain was once again in the forest, and it traveled with a chill through the breeze. The leaves waved overhead, and the branches swayed with each gust, which Argo felt cut through him.

He held Wander's good paw in his hand. It was small and black and fit perfectly into his palm. He ran his thumb over her sharp nails and soft pad, which had been covered in scratches. She looked up at him and slowly closed her eyes, falling fast asleep again.

"I'm sorry, girl," he whispered. "We need to keep going." He stood and mindfully rolled the knapsack back over her, then lifted her onto his back. "Let's just follow this trail," he told her once she was settled. "It's really all we can do."

The path had been churned up by footprints and horse hooves and could clearly be seen through the lively grass, and the sight gave him the confidence he needed to keep following it. The sound of light rain traveling through the Woods far away slowly crept toward them, then finally overcame and passed over them. The water collected on the canopy high above them and fell sporadically in large and heavy droplets.

Argo rearranged his pack and pulled his cloak up and over it. Then he loosened the tie which held it together in front of him. Now Wander's head poked through the same opening as his. He pulled the hood over them both, and she wiggled her nose to the side and poked it out of the opening, just above his shoulder.

The muddy path became even stickier with the rain, and his steps became heavier, each one giving slightly more than the last. His thighs burned with each footstep from the added weight, so he stepped off the path and walked alongside it in the grass, trudging through the wildlife and leaving an obvious trail behind them. The path wound near several small streams which were flowing heavily with the rain. It reminded him of the traumatic experience of the rapids. He stopped at one of these, which was opened wide and shallow, for Wander to drink from. She lapped slowly, then turned her muzzle away. Her strength was failing her. As she struggled, a terrible burden came over Argo—that he'd been responsible for hurting her.

She needs help or she's not going to make it.

He put her back underneath his cloak and stepped over the running water. Off in the distance of the other side, they saw bright colors littering the forest floor. First one, then another, then masses of wildflowers overtaking the soft grass. They were in various hues of purples, red, oranges, yellows, greens, and many others, with some rising to the height of his knees and painting a riot of colors across the landscape. His steps were leaving footprints across them as he walked, so he stepped once more back on the trail. His foot sank almost to his ankle. Each step from there felt immense, yet he continued, comforted by the beauty around him. The trees were ever as high and yet farther separated than before, with the colorful groves of wildflowers carpeting the distance between them. Through the light rain, he spotted a hollowed-out root system under a tree which offered cover from the rain and time to rest for a moment.

He stepped off the path and made his way over. The large roots opened up to a hollow in the tree, similar to the last one they'd rested in, but much bigger. This one was elevated enough off the ground to keep them out of the mud. He cautiously stepped inside and examined it, then placed Wander against the far wall of the small hollow. She looked exhausted and feverish from her broken paw. He took off his sword and bow and squeezed next to her, bringing his knees up to his chest so he could fit entirely under without being exposed to the rain. There they sat, watching the rain fall drearily on the wildflowers from the safety of their hollow.

The melodic rhythm of the rain fell like a sweet lullaby. The dry warmth of the hollow comforted him, and he felt strangely at ease. His eyes grew heavy, and he slumped back against Wander, who was quietly snoring. Without either of them noticing, a hypnosis had pulled them into a deep slumber.

CHAPTER 33

The Dream

Argo sat on a bench back in his village's town square. Clouds of gray blanketed the sky in all directions. The air was warm and wet, as it often was during those early mornings, and the wooden bench beneath him had soaked through from an earlier rain. He could smell the earthy richness from the mud beneath them.

Villagers packed the square shoulder to shoulder. They pushed past each other as they walked to finish their daily errands, their movement blurring their faces. Their clothes were of different shades of gray that matched the color of the sky above them, each person nearly indistinguishable from the last, and they moved like waves in a stormy sea.

A man sat beside him on the bench. Argo turned and saw it was his father. Together, they surveyed the mass of the crowd, saying nothing to each other as they watched each passerby like two sailors from a shoreline.

His father reached beside him and pulled out a loaf of warm bread wrapped in a cloth, tore off a piece, and gave it to his son. Steam rose from the soft inside with a heavenly, yeasty scent. Argo took a large bite and let the taste linger. The homely sensation melted away in his mouth. He chewed it slowly, and it was everything he needed. They continued to share the meal until his father tore off the last of the bread and held it out for his son, who ate it in one bite. When he finished, he looked at his father, who gazed tenderly back at him. He placed his large hand firmly on Argo's shoulder, and with an affectionate and dutiful smile, he stood up and vanished into the crowd.

Argo stood up to stop him, but he was already gone. He ran desperately into the crowd after him, frantically searching, but the sea of people overwhelmed and tossed and turned him like the tides. He pushed, begged, and pleaded for people to let him through, to let him cut a path, but his cries fell on deaf ears. No one could hear him. The more he tried to stand in place, the harder the crowd pushed against him. He pushed and shoved until he could no longer take it and was forced to move with them. He yelled out over the crowd, calling for his father. More and more, the crowd pushed against him. No matter how hard he fought, the people overpowered him. Enraged, he pushed blindly at the crowd. "Get back!" he shouted as loud as he could. "Get off me, damn you! Let me go!"

He pushed again and again until he was giving blows and tearing at the crowd like a rabid animal, twisting and clawing his way through. Each blow sent bodies tumbling, yet the crowd flowed over the bodies as if nothing had happened. He held his arms out and stood on some of the bodies he'd knocked down so he could see over the crowd. There was the bench he and his father had broken bread over, only now it wasn't empty. His friends Abaddon and Castor stood on the bench, staring directly at Argo. Castor had his bow in hand with an arrow knocked, and Abaddon stood while running his thumb across the blade of his knife. Argo stared at them curiously, then was fiercely pulled off his perch. He cried at the top of his lungs, and bodies cast themselves ceaselessly upon him until he slammed against the muddy ground. His lungs collapsed under the force, the crushing weight of the crowd choking him, and his heart couldn't beat any longer. He cried again and pushed as hard as he could against the sea, but he'd been taken—

Argo snapped awake. Beads of sweat dripped from his forehead into his eyes. He looked out of the hollow and through the thick rain. A loud crack tore in the distance. He froze in place. Wander's eyes shot open, and her ears perked up; she was too weak to move anymore.

That sounded like a tree limb cracking. He sifted through his mind for possible explanations. *Did the beast follow us?*

As delicately as he could, he leaned over and grabbed his bow and arrows, careful not to let them rattle and make any sound. Then he grabbed his sword and carefully unsheathed it in his other hand. He ran through the situation in his mind.

I could stay in here and fight, but something that was out to endanger me could easily have the advantage. But if the sound was deliberate, it could be used to lure me out of my hiding place. It may have just been the rain. Though if someone followed us, the rain may have covered our tracks. And if I go outside, I'll lose any protection and shelter from the hollow, but it would give me greater freedom of movement and allow me to use my bow. I can't fight back in here.

Weighing the considerations carefully, he peered his head out of the opening and looked around. The thick raindrops beat against his hood in dense beads. The forest seemed as empty as it had been, though an unnerving stillness permeated it. The birds stopped singing, and all the sounds stopped. He looked down the trail first left, then right, and saw nothing. The path carried on until it passed out of sight.

The rain fell even harder than before and limited the visibility further. Argo cocked his head to the side and listened. Despite the rain beating against the canopy and falling to the foliage beneath, the forest felt eerily quiet but not empty.

Knock!

Something hit a tree somewhere behind him. He knew the sound immediately and instantly tucked away his sword and knocked an arrow in his bow. In one motion, he rose out of the hollow at full draw and turned in the direction of the sound.

Nothing.

His senses screamed. The unnerving feeling that he was being preyed upon simmered inside him. He quickly scanned the area with his bow still drawn, looking for any anomaly in the tree line while slowly creeping toward the direction of the sound.

The forest screamed louder in its haunting silence.

His steps were light and deliberate and fell mute on the rain-soaked wildflowers.

Ahead of him, he noticed something light in the dead center of a tree. Argo inched closer, still scanning the forest until he was finally close enough to touch the tree. He raised his hand against the bark. An area the size of two fingers was missing; something had scraped that bit of bark away. He looked down and saw an imprint in the wildflowers surrounding the tree. A large tree limb had fallen and crushed the flowers beneath it. Still watching his surroundings, Argo moved cautiously closer to the fallen timber.

The thick raindrops were breaking against the limb which had been carefully cut away from the tree by hand until its own deadweight sent it crashing down below.

The forest shuffled behind him. He snapped around and pulled his bow to a full draw. The forest was still empty.

Suddenly he heard Wander wail loudly from the hollow. "Wander!" he cried out, running as fast as he could back to the tree. Then he stopped cold in his tracks.

Abaddon rose from the hollow, holding the knapsack with Wander.

"Abaddon?" Argo asked, surprised, lowering his bow.

Abaddon's face was scratched and distressed. His wet and flat hair fell over his eyes, and his clothes were matted and torn, exposing a web of cuts and scrapes. His blood bled through his once-white shirt and stained it in dark brown patches.

"Argo," he said with a sinister look in his eyes. The rain dripped down his face and soaked through his tattered clothes.

"What are you doing here? What are you doing with Wander?" Argo asked nervously.

Abaddon seemed to choke on his words, as though fighting back the urge to spill his thoughts forth. "You're coming with me. We're going back," he finally said quietly. "I told you that you shouldn't have come."

"Why are you here?" Argo demanded loudly.

"We're going back, Argo," he repeated slowly. "The village sent me to bring you back." Abaddon spoke in a way Argo had never heard him speak before.

"What?" Argo asked in shock. "Go back? I'm not going back, Abaddon, why would I go back now?"

"Why?" Abaddon asked sarcastically. "Because Emerick and Castor are dead because of you."

"Castor? What happened?" Argo demanded, taking a step closer.

"A beast killed him. With the body of a great boar and antlers for tusks." Abaddon's voice rose sharply. He gritted his teeth fiercely, and he pointed at Argo as he spoke. The words which had been long boiling somewhere deep inside him came spewing out, one after another. "We came in looking for you. That's why I look like this. The beast rushed us, and he was gored and died in my arms. It was because of you. You deprived him of his death with The Rider."

A grave sense of disbelief swept over Argo. He didn't want to believe it. *This has to be some cruel lie.* He'd never seen anyone gored before, but he was well familiar with how ghastly it could be. "I never asked you to come find me. Don't put his death on me."

"No. The village made us," he replied sharply. "They held a meeting the night you left and sent us to come find you. Emeric would've come too, but he traveled that very night. His leg was rotting, and The Rider came for him."

Argo remembered how he'd turned around that first night and seen the village gathered together. *They must have passed right by me.*

"Why would they hold a meeting? Why would they care?" Argo asked, taking another step forward.

"Everyone cares now, Argo. You're disrupting the balance. The order of death. No one knows if you can actually kill The Rider, but they're scared because you're trying. What happens when you anger him? What happens, Argo, when you throw his gift of a peaceful death back at him? You might as well spit in his face when you meet him."

"What am I supposed to do, Abaddon?" Argo asked. "Keep the cycle going of living and dying? For how long? What's the purpose of it?"

A rolling sound of thunder cracked high above them and echoed through the Woods. They both stopped and listened to it.

"That is the purpose, Argo. We live, we die, and we go somewhere else after. What more are you looking for?" Abaddon replied.

Argo remembered the ferryman's words to him—that people can only understand what's in their capacity to understand. It was never as evident as it was now, seeing his friend beaten and standing before him, holding Wander hostage. The rain beat against her face, and she tucked her head into the pack as much as she could.

Argo shook his head slowly in denial. "How easy it is to stand there and judge. Rule over the lives of others. Have them live how you would have lived. A life ruled by fear. It's a rot, and it's taken hold of all of you, down to the very roots and into your core. And just like a rot, you can't rest until you infect everything else the same." Argo's voice carried over the sound of the pouring rain. He felt himself rise within as he had only felt a few times in his life. "If anything, it only strengthens me to keep going in order to avoid this plague you call life. Now this rot, which all of you harbor so deep inside, has pulled itself to the surface and shown you who you really are. Scared and selfish. It wasn't me that had Castor killed. It was all of you and your fear. You just needed someone to blame!" His shoulders were drawn back, and he stood defiantly. He took another few steps forward.

Abaddon drew his knife and put it against Wander's neck. She was too weak to respond to the cold blade. "Stop, Argo," he demanded harshly. "No closer." He nervously ran his thumb across the blade.

"Put that away," Argo ordered, not as confidently this time. "You're going to kill my dog to try to bring me back?"

Abaddon started to tear up. The knife shook wildly at Wander's throat. "Come back, Argo! I don't want to do this. You need to come back with me. Please," he cried out. Tears rolled down his face and were lost in the rain.

Argo saw the instability rising in his friend's quivering hand. He'd never once seen him like this, not in all their long years together. "Abaddon, put her down. It's going to be okay. This isn't you." He held out his hands and took another small step closer.

"No. It's not. But this is what you've made us, Argo. All of us," he cried.

His expression was hard for Argo to see, and it brought him to tears as well. "All of who? Our village?" Nothing had ever felt more unnatural than making his friend feel this way.

Abaddon wiped away his tears with his wet sleeve, revealing his swollen, red eyes. "They took your father. They told me to tell you that if you don't come back, they'll kill him. By midnight of your day, if you don't—"

Wander suddenly kicked, and Abaddon almost fumbled her, but he held on to his hostage. "If you don't come back, they're going to send him into the forest for him to die the same as you." Abaddon's face was flustered. His eyes and cheeks were swollen from emotion, and he held hate and discontent in his words. "They took my family too. And Castor's. Said they'll kill them as well if we don't return with you." He barely got the sentence out before looking away, holding back another wave of tears. "And now Castor'll never come back." He broke down as he uttered the words and crouched down, supporting himself on the ground with his hand still holding the knife. He wiped away the tears again but couldn't stop them from coming.

The words hit Argo like a blow to the chest. His stomach sank, and a cold chill crept down his arms and up his neck, gripping him in terror. He'd never once expected the village to act like this, and now Abaddon's motive seemed clear and true.

Am I the enemy?

The fruit of his ambitions had now bloomed to the demise of all he knew.

Did I draw them to this, or did I just reveal what was hidden beneath the whole time?

He took a step back and fell to his knees, bracing himself with his bow hand on the ground. The strength had fled from him, and he felt as if he was going to pass out.

He needed a moment. If he could have a moment to take a step back and reexamine his plan, he'd be okay. He'd felt so justified and righteous. *How did it grow into this?*

The Woods in all their greatness were now mesmerizingly chaotic and swallowed him in its clutches. He felt hopeless, a feeling which had been dripping on his heart but was now released like a torrent onto him. He felt anger toward Abaddon, anger toward his village and his home, and anger toward himself most of all. He breathed heavily against his own will and focused all of his attention on his breathe, and with every rise and fall of his chest, he felt life surge within him. He cleaned his face and looked up at his friend, who watched him with just as much bitterness.

Argo stuck his bow in the ground and leaned his weight against it to stand. It shook and bent beneath him, then slid out from under him. He fell toward a tree and hit hard against it. He braced himself against it with his hand, then slowly rose to his feet. They felt weak under him and his knees were going to give out. He wiped the mud off himself deliberately and pushed himself off the tree to stand on his own. "Look at you, Abaddon. Look at all of you. Did I make this of you? Or did I just show you who you really are?" The rain and tears dripped down his face and into his mouth. He spat them out. "This is not my village. Look at what you've become. Here you stand, my closest friend, with your knife at my innocent dog's throat. Look at her," Argo demanded of his friend. He pointed to Wander in his arms. "Look her in the eyes. She had nothing but love for you. Now you look at her and tell me that this is who you are. Look at her!" Tears poured uncontrollably from his eyes once again.

Wander lay in the pack, her head resting heavily on Abaddon, and her eyes were half open in a daze of sleepy awareness, too sick and weak to put up a struggle.

Abaddon stared hopelessly into Argo's eyes. Tears welled to the surface, about to break at any moment. His lips tightened and curled, and his face strained fiercely against his sea of emotion. He shook nervously, then broke his gaze with Argo and turned away, looking away from them both.

*****

Abaddon forced himself to look into Wander's eyes, and the sight of innocence and all that's right in this world broke him. It broke him down to his soul and shattered his will. He'd never seen anything so beautiful and sweet and loving in his arms, had never in all his time and experiences with Wander seen her in this light. Not once had he seen the innocent beauty and unconditional love that dog had for him, a man not even her master but just a member of the company she kept.

No. This wasn't him. Argo and Wander had shattered him into a million pieces, leaving him cold and crumbled and destroyed and hateful of even himself. He was once so righteous in his quest. Now he broke again into tears. His face clenched and wretched in agony at the sight of the knife in his hands. Immediately, he released his grip and the blade plunged to the ground, where it struck forcefully upright.

The moment became clear. Nothing was simply black and white. There was no good or evil, which the two of them had dreamed of so clearly. There were only shades of gray. They were arguing over an ambiguous question which had no right answer. The right path was as forlorn and twisted as the trees they had ventured so deep into. Truth and moral duty were only a matter of perspective, and the two friends were spinning desperately from these, one into the other, seamlessly yet so distant from one another.

Abaddon noticed that the evening had crept up on them, and night would be there soon. "Don't move," he demanded of Argo. He carefully set Wander down beside him and pulled his own pack in front of him, removing a torch and a flintstone. The torch was wrapped in an oiled cloth to protect it in case of rain. He looked up at Argo again. "I mean it. Don't make any move. This is for both of us."

He vigilantly drew his cloak over his arm and shielded the items from the rain, then, propping it up with his knee, he skillfully unwrapped the torch, struck the flintstone, and started the fire with a single strike. His torch erupted into flame, illuminating the pocket he'd created with his cloak and body. He let the flame breath and gain strength dangerously close to him, then he slowly pulled back his cloak and exposed it to the elements. It stayed lit and beat against the downpour.

Argo finally broke the silence. "We would never make it in time. It's too late."

"The village is no more than a few hours away. Just through the Woods," Abaddon retorted.

Argo looked at him curiously. "What about the cave? The tunnels? The valley?"

Abaddon looked confused. "What are you talking about? We entered the Woods yesterday morning and followed your tracks on the path straight here. There was no cave, nor tunnels, nor valley," he answered.

"Then how…?"

"The Woods work in strange ways, Argo. You know this perhaps better than anyone else," Abaddon added as he picked up Wander. The Woods were rapidly descending into darkness, and the only light was that of Abaddon's torch, which whipped strongly against the rain.

"Take your torch and go back home," Argo ordered Abaddon. "Tell whatever tale you need to."

Abaddon thought silently for a moment, unsure of what to say.

"I only ask this," Argo said. "Take Wander with you. I don't expect that she has much longer to live with her wounds. Still, it is a better fate than what lies ahead for me. Do it for her."

"No." He shook his head. "You come with me. Take Wander yourself and travel with me. You're nothing here without the torchlight," he responded. "You know that."

The rain and clouds obscured all the light other than the torch, though he could see Argo working through his proposal. If he did come across The Rider, he'd have no chance of fighting without it. Argo could continue to press his stubbornness, but to what end? Abaddon knew that if he had accepted his terms and left, then Argo would be here alone and in the dark in the pouring rain. He could try and make a fire, but it would be near impossible with the constant wet, and even if he managed a fire, that would be difficult to fashion into an efficient torch. He would prove a point at a moot and desperate cost.

Abbadon watched the flames light up the increasingly dark forest. If Argo accepted, he would go with Abaddon, have Wander back, and have the torchlight. The unknown factor would be the Woods, which seem to have plans of their own. An unpredictable and incalculable element of fate already had them in its grip.

Abaddon stood quietly and watched his friend intently think through the offer.

"All right," Argo said. "You give me Wander, and I'll go with you. We leave our fate to the Woods. If we make it back to the village, then so be it. If not, and we meet some other fate, then so be it as well." The situation wasn't ideal, but it was the best compromise either of them had.

"Let the Woods decide." Argo declared. "As you said, this place works in mysterious ways, and I have a feeling that we don't have much say in it at this point. And Abaddon, I would like to decide to walk with you once more as a friend and not a foe, as we currently stand."

Abaddon tearfully nodded and laid Wander down.

CHAPTER 34

The Friend

Argo and Abaddon walked as friends once again. The rain slowed to a steady drizzle and could be heard striking and passing through the canopy high above them. The torchlight beat against the black night and gave off a small glow of wild orange and yellow, enough for them to make out the muddy path beneath them, which they walked to the side of to avoid sinking into the mud. The high grass and wildflowers brushed against their legs with each step, and their trouser legs stuck heavily to them. Each breath was dense and wet, and the once-crisp air of the Woods felt thicker, as if the forest as a whole had been compressed slightly.

They exchanged tales of their journeys as they traveled. Argo explained how he had been turned around by the Woods and seen the village gathered on that first night, and then of his encounter with the antlered beast, and of Silas the Crow and The Tree Traveler, and of the ferryman who once loved The Lady of the Woods. Abaddon was entirely captivated by the story and kept asking questions, driving them down further and further to every last detail. He hung on each of his friend's words.

Then Abaddon explained his side of the tale. He spoke of how the village fell into chaos, how Emeric had suddenly been called to travel, how he and Castor were tasked with bringing Argo back, and how shortly after entering the Woods, they encountered the antlered beast that had killed their friend.

Argo listened and asked no further questions, only shook his head and let his friend speak. It hurt him to hear. The discussion slowly faded, and moments passed where he wanted to break the silence and continue speaking to Argo, but each time, he withdrew his decision and allowed the strange-yet-comforting ambience to continue. They trudged through the rainy darkness with only the dim light of the torch to lead the way.

Abaddon daydreamed of returning to his village and to his home, where the hearth was warm and dry. Flashes of the village folk praising him as a hero and a savior filled his mind, and as much as he fought against it, he slowly became intoxicated by the idea. He imagined how everyone would look at him, how the tides of fate forced his hand and ironically created his own tale in which he was the hero. For once, he was the one who performed the brave deed.

Like an arrow to his chest, another thought pierced his mind. He remembered his family being held hostage. The same people who would revere him as a hero and tell his tale were also holding those he loved so dearly. The idea fostered sourly. Why should he care about their opinions? About their praise?

"They can all be damned for this." Abaddon thought to himself. *"For Castor. For the Lady of the Woods and even Argo's father—what was he supposed to do against his only son's dying wishes?"* He clenched his fist slightly at the thought. *"They can all be damned..."*

He would've done this deed all the same, if they'd approached him kindly. If only they had acknowledged what he was—a strong, intelligent man who would have saved the village if they had only asked. But they didn't bother. As soon as word was out of Argo's fate, the village collective digressed into a death mob spewing ideas, each suggestion worse than the last. As much as Abaddon resented Argo for all of this, he could never admit that he understood. Abaddon had felt the poison of fear not only in himself but also in those moments as a village.

"Argo was right. It wasn't us and it wasn't me. It isn't me."

He turned back and saw Argo in the torchlight behind him, walking with his gaze focused on each step, Wander asleep on his back and under the cover of his cloak. For the first time, through the hazy rain and dim light of the torch, Abaddon saw Argo for who he really was—just an average man, not particularly strong nor tall nor special in any physical way. Even with this, Argo radiated an energy of absolute magnificence. He'd become something more, even if he hadn't realized it yet himself. He was no longer the same friend who'd stepped into the forest just mere days ago. He'd become refined, had metamorphosed into this evolved being; something which Abaddon knew he wasn't. He both hated Argo and admired him for it.

***

Argo couldn't see much through the shadows leading him. He watched Abaddon's steps and tried to follow each one, sinking slightly into each depression left in his wake. His thoughts drifted as well, and he felt a strange comfort in his mediation, knowing that he had no true destination in mind. He hadn't the faintest idea where they were walking, or if the forest would spit them out at the foot of the tree line and into the village, and he was perfectly fine with either.

If that's it, then so be it.

The idea of fate no longer being in his apparent control was comforting. He felt an uncanny relief in the solace that he didn't have to make another decision on where to go or which path to take. He'd given the control to his friend and his torch, and perhaps most importantly to the forest itself. He thought of themselves as though in the midst of a great and powerful river, its current taking him precisely where it intended. He had swum; he had fought; and now he was in it.

Abaddon stopped suddenly in front of him, causing Argo to nearly run into him. He lowered his torch and looked away from the light and gazed into the darkness.

Argo had seen him do this several times on their early morning hunting trips and late night returns. He was allowing his eyes to adjust to the night so he could gauge how much illumination was given off from the moon. However, tonight there was none. Through the high trees above, the rain now came down softly like a fine mist from the thick clouds overhead, which loomed over them and blocked the moonlight.

"What time do you think it is?" Argo asked.

Abaddon observed the area around them. "Not sure. Midnight can't be too far off though." He moved the torch back in front of him and motioned for Argo to follow. "Let's go, we need to keep moving." He took a step forward, then stopped in his tracks.

Wanders ear perked up.

Argo instantly halted. They were both completely still, frozen in time, listening. His heart raced, and his blood coursed violently through his veins. Off in the distance, he heard it. Off in the distance, he felt it.

Abaddon bounded quietly to a nearby tree and jabbed his knife into it. The blade stuck firm and deep into the bark. He placed his ear on the hilt and covered it with his hand.

Argo and Wander watched him nervously.

His eyes shot open, "Hooves! The Rider!" he whispered loudly. "Run!"

Wander shook her head out from beneath the cloak. She must've heard the sound in the distance as well.

They ran at a dead sprint down the trail. They heard the beating hooves of the mount racing behind them, heavy strides that struck the earth mightily with every step. The Rider hunted them.

With each one of their steps, their feet sank into the mud as if it were struggling to consume them, but still they fought. Wander bounced furiously back and forth on her master's back as they ran desperately. The light of the torch tossed and turned and threw its light across the blackness, waving in and out of the path, lighting it one second and abandoning it the next. The rain had stopped. A cool breeze now returned, cutting bitterly through their wet clothing as they desperately ran through it.

They broke through the field of wildflowers, leaving a trail blazed through the long stems behind them. The path wound and twisted around the trees and over their roots. Mud flew up behind them as they kicked it up. Abaddon stepped in a hole and flew across the ground. His sword jammed into the mud and stuck upright; his body contorted around it. The torch flew forward and landed in the wet grass, still burning dimly.

Argo ran over to him and picked him up by his arms. The racing hooves were growing louder behind them. "Go!" he commanded Abaddon, who stumbled forward covered in mud and picked up his torch without breaking a stride.

They ran as fast as their feet could take them, jumping over roots and dodging what branches they could see.

"Up there!" Abaddon shouted to Argo, still racing ahead of him. "It's an opening!"

The hooves were right on them, yet neither dared to look back.

They fled for the opening as quickly as they could. They were so close that they could feel the air opening.

Finally, they broke through, still not daring to look back.

Abaddon found his speed and took off significantly faster than before. Argo sprinted wearily behind, unable to keep up.

They were now clear of the mud and in a large, open meadow carpeted with a sea of the wildflowers, each illuminated beautifully in blueish-white fluorescents like those in the grove in the cave. Another small stream, surrounded by high grass, cut through the side of the wildflowers. The sky revealed a gorgeous full moon, closer and fuller than Argo had ever seen before. It parted the clouds, revealing the vast ocean of stars beyond.

The tree line in front of them was a good distance away, and they were fighting for every inch. Argo didn't know to what end they were running, only that the tree line was where they needed to be, but suddenly, he tripped on something in the high flowers and fell harshly, landing directly on his stomach. Wander was thrown forward from his pack and tumbled forcefully in front of him. She wailed loudly at the pain.

Abaddon immediately stopped and turned toward him. "Argo!" he yelled from a distance ahead.

Argo rolled over and finally looked behind them. A distance behind, a Rider in ghastly black garb galloped at full speed. He took no light from the moon or from the flowers, as if he were only a passing shadow. He rode his nightmarish mount, his form frightfully grim and strong, as gracefully as if he were gliding across the night sky. A long broadsword waved up and down from his side as he rode. His horse's armor remained black as the abyss. It rattled coldly with every heavy and thunderous stride.

Argo felt each step shake the earth beneath him. Abaddon froze, watching The Rider burn through their tracks.

At breakneck speed, The Rider veered off the trail in a dead sprint and circled around their right flank, as if to cut them off.

Argo traced The Rider across the landscape, mesmerized by his every moment. Abaddon stood deathly still as he circled their position. Argo stumbled over to Wander, who was still sprawled across the ground. Together they watched The Rider sprint ahead and ride in a large circle around them, keeping his unnerving speed and poise.

The small party stood completely still, dreadfully watching his every move.

After a full circle, The Rider pulled back on the reins and brought his mare to stop on the trail they had just blazed. The mount reared on his back legs and cried out loudly. His silhouette stood tall against the moonlit sky.

They were all still. Argo looked at Abaddon, and their eyes met from the large distance between them. Their chests were rising and collapsing painfully from their pursuit. Abaddon, too tired to remain standing, leaned over and rested his hands on his knees. His eyes met Argo's, who was now huddled over Wander. They stared at one another in a powerful silence, eyes locked, coated with sweat and mud, still soaked to the bone.

Abaddon rose and looked at The Rider, who sat menacingly still atop his mount. Then he looked back at his friend and his companion. Argo saw in his friends eyes a terror he'd never seen in a man. They were wide open and screamed of fear. His mouth wanted to utter words but only trembled. His hands and knees shook violently.

Without a word, Abaddon backed away slowly.

***

Finally, Abaddon turned and broke into a sprint down the path and toward the tree line away from his best friend. He mustered all the strength he had and ran from the friend he loved, admired, and looked up to, the friend he had set out courageously to retrieve and return. He turned his back on fate, on The Rider he was one day destined to meet, and most importantly, on the one he had once thought a brother. He ran, and those who remained in the meadow watched him vanish into the trees.

CHAPTER 35

The Rider

The cool breeze sailed gently across the meadow, caressing the sea of illuminated flowers gently in its wake. The two were now alone, man and Rider. Argo looked at Wander, who looked back at him. He shook her playfully one last time on her head and gave her a kiss on her forehead, the same place he'd always kissed her since she was a puppy.

Powerful feelings rose from deep inside him and found their way to his eyes, where tears collected densely and fell under their own weight, landing drop by drop on his beloved friend and loyal companion who was with him now in the end. He tore himself away and rose to his feet, dutifully facing his foe.

The Rider sat stoically upon his mount, watching him without a move.

Argo stared back at him, though he could only see the pitch-dark outline. A cold dread overtook Argo like a frozen poison beating its way through his body. He let his pack fall to the ground. Next, he removed his bow and quiver, which he placed neatly on top of his pack. He untied the knot of his cloak and laid it out as best as he could across the ground, then caringly picked up Wander and placed her on it. Then he folded it once more around her to keep her warm.

With tears in his eyes, he looked back at The Rider and unhitched his sword, still in its sheath, from behind his back and held it in front of him. He withdrew the blade clumsily and placed the sheath carefully next to his bow, then rose again, holding the blade out, ready to receive his opponent.

The Rider kept watching from atop his mount.

The moonlight shone brightly upon them now, and the night had become quieter than it had ever been. Only the sound of the wind rustling through the flowers carried through the cool night.

Finally, the nightmarish mount stepped forward. A heavy hoof hit the ground, and the armor clad together tightly. With each harrowing step, The Rider drew closer.

Argo stood where he was and felt the pain of each step as if it were landing on him and not the ground.

The Rider drew nearer and stopped in front of Argo, the moonlight draping his towering form and his mount like a blanket and casting a long, dark shadow over the wildflowers. Behind his saddle rested a thick burlap sack, which draped across the hindquarters of the beast.

The sword shook wildly in Argo's hands, which felt as if they could give out at any moment.

They stared at one another in the silence.

Argo's arms were now quivering out of control from the exhaustion of holding his sword out. Was there something he was supposed to say, or some proper way to greet The Rider that he'd maybe forgotten? He'd seen him numerous times before from a distance, but he'd never heard any of the exchanges.

"I received your letter," Argo stuttered, "and I'm here."

The Rider stoically looked down upon him from his mount. "I know who you are, Argo. You have been the subject of great discussion as of late." His articulate voice echoed deeply, an eerie mix of intellect and intimidation that traveled in an unearthly tone through the meadow. It sounded as if it weren't bound by the limitations of this world but instead bridged the gap between this one and another. It was also strangely human or had remnants of a human's past, lost yet still present beneath the surface.

"Unintentionally," Argo answered nervously. He felt as if he would collapse under his own weight and crumble right there in front of The Rider.

"Unintentionally?" The Rider asked calmly. "Was it not you who chose to enter these woods and seek me?"

"It was. I didn't expect all of this to happen," he answered.

"What did you expect to happen?" The Rider asked. "You have upset the order of death. Is it wrong of your people to restore it? To keep the world in its balance?"

On top of all the emotions he felt, Argo now felt an immense guilt and shame "I…" He couldn't finish his statement. "I understand."

"Have I not given your people the gift of a painless death? Have I not answered their prayers?" he asked Argo.

"You have," Argo said, ashamed.

"Then why refuse it?" The Rider asked.

Argo didn't answer. He looked to the ground, searching for the right answer, but only one came to him. "I needed something more."

"Something more?" The Rider questioned.

"What's the point of all of this? What's the point of living ten years, or one hundred years, or even one thousand years?" Now the words spilled out of him naturally. "I don't know what life was like before your visits. All I know is what I've been told, and even that's not much. But what I've heard were tales of bravery, of adventure, of love. Something more than… well, something more than this."

The Rider shifted his weight, and his mount sidestepped in return, though he said nothing.

"I looked at my life," Argo continued, "and I saw it wasting away. It was the same old day over and over again while my face and body grew older. You gave us an easy death, which is an amazing gift in itself, but in return, it robbed us of so much more. People live in fear—fear to take chances and fear to love or explore or make something greater of themselves. Life's no more than a waiting game for your letter. Whatever lies at the other end of this forest, wherever you take your travelers… that must be real life. That must be where all this matters, right?"

The Rider looked at him.

Argo stood, waiting.

Finally, The Rider spoke. "Did you find something more?"

Argo thought for a moment, then nodded. "Yes."

The Rider remained stoic in front of him, and after another moment, he carefully shifted his weight and dismounted gracefully from his horse, as if a statue had come alive and broken its mold. He moved with a heavy slowness, as if he'd awoken from a deep sleep. His feet hit the ground with a mighty force worthy of a man thrice his size. At his side was a longsword in a dark leather sheath, which swayed as he stepped closer to Argo, who remained in place and kept his footing. His mount cautiously backed away from his master.

The rumors were true. The Rider stood higher and stronger than any man Argo had ever seen. He placed his chainmail hand on the hilt of his sword as he stepped closer to Argo. The moonlight cast his great shadow across Argo, who was now shaking in terror. Even now at this close distance, The Rider was as ominous as ever. Every feature was buried away in the shadows. All that remained was the massive colossus that carried in every movement the gravity of a falling tree. He stopped at a dueling distance from Argo, who held his blade once more in front of him.

The Rider stood still and ominous, his hand resting on the hilt of his sword.

Argo broke his gaze and looked quickly at Wander, who watched wearily from beneath the cloak, still too weak to move. A small shadow cast across the cloak as her tail wagged eagerly from beneath its weight.

With a tight and articulate movement, The Rider reached across with his other hand and gripped the hilt of his sword. Each finger curled and fell into a firm grip.

Argo was ready to run at any moment but he held his posture.

The Rider stared at Argo, then drew the blade out in one long, smooth motion. The sword was as black as the rest of him. He extended it outright, surgically splitting the light from the moon.

Argo's knees shook violently beneath him, threatening to give out. His hands felt so sweaty, he thought his sword was going to slide right out between them, so he gripped even harder, bleaching his knuckles as white as the moonlight.

The two swordsmen faced one another, blades outstretched. The Rider sidestepped to the right.

Argo matched him.

Then another step, and another, almost as a courtesy dance, mirroring each other's movement. The bright moon now rested behind Argo and fell upon The Rider, who passed through the light as if it belonged to him. The gentle breeze still blew around them, and the illuminated wildflowers between them ebbed and flowed as the ocean.

The Rider stopped moving.

Argo was paralyzed in fear yet stopped as well.

"There is an invisible thread that ties us together, Argo. Between a man and his fate."

Argo lowered his blade, unsure of how to take the words.

"Your friend is watching. Strike me down," The Rider said as he raised his blade high into the night sky.

Sensing an attack, Argo sidestepped and raised his sword over his head to deflect the blow.

The Rider brought his sword down fiercely. It clashed with a tremendous ring against Argo's blade, then slid off to the side.

The blow was magnificent. He'd never felt such a force against him.

The Rider's blade fell and almost hit the ground. He stopped it right before it did, then pulled it back and whirled his arms in a wild motion, swinging the pitch-black blade across him.

Argo watched and threw himself down suddenly beneath it. The Rider's movements were slow and powerful, but the blade whistled above his head. He felt it slice through the air, deadly in its act. He lost his balance and fell backward onto the grass.

The Rider took another step forward, and in one motion he took a swing and followed its momentum back over his head, bringing it straight down over Argo, who saw the attack and tossed himself to the side. The sword struck the ground with an immeasurable force and dug itself deep into the dirt.

Argo's eyes shot open wide, and he gasped as it landed. He backed away from his foe and clumsily stood back up.

The Rider looked at him and heaved his blade from the earth, dragging up dirt along with the weapon's tip. Still looking at Argo, he whipped his sword behind him. The mud slid off the blade and threw itself across the meadow. They stood face-to-face once more.

The Rider's mount backpedaled again, and Wander barked loudly from her resting place.

They sidestepped and sidestepped again, back in the rhythm of the dance.

Argo knew that if he wanted to win, he needed to attack.

The Rider stepped closer again, closing the distance between them. He raised his sword mightily above his head to strike down, but Argo rushed forward and sliced across The Rider's exposed abdomen.

The Rider curled over and dropped his blade, which stuck vertically upright into the mud. He fell to his knees and clutched his stomach, staring at the empty space in the moonlight where his foe had stood.

Argo turned in disbelief at his fallen enemy. The Rider never looked back at him. Instead, he remained on his knees, facing where Argo had once stood. His blade stood upright in the flowers, their petals brushed against the cold metal. Argo kept his guard up, in shock at what he'd done. His sword was held outright toward The Rider, as if to fend away a sudden counterattack.

The Rider collapsed to the ground.

In the forest ahead, a loud tumble came from the trees, and a string of canopies shook themselves along the trail, and then all was quiet.

CHAPTER 36

The Dead

Argo stared in disbelief at the corpse on the ground in front of him. A powerful wave of relief and awe overcame him. He dropped his sword and buried his face in his hands to shut out the world around him. Collapsing to his knees and then farther to the ground, he wailed from the emotion overriding him. The gravity of the situation had yet to sink in, yet he felt its weight nonetheless. In a single instant, a swing of his sword had changed everything. Life would never be the same, nor could it go back to what it was.

He pulled back his hands which were covered in tears, mud, and sweat. He was no longer the young man who'd entered the forest; he'd become something else entirely, something he didn't recognize and deep down even feared. His hands were tainted red in the blood he'd spilled from a conscious being, however much so The Rider was. He'd never killed another life who could speak to him, much less one he'd had a conversation with. He felt no reward. No proud sense of accomplishment or overwhelming joy. He felt rotted down to his core that he had destroyed something beautiful and, in turn, destroyed that part of himself with it. All along, this was precisely what he'd asked for. The goal he'd set out to accomplish.

He hated himself and what he'd done. Tears poured down his cheeks. He sat up hopelessly and stared at the lifeless body sprawled out before him. The sound of the softly flowing stream picked up in the distance, and the songs of the night wildlife had returned. Crickets chirped and frogs croaked, and just like that, life carried on.

He looked at Wander still lying under his cloak, which rose and sank with each one of her slow, laborious breaths. He struggled to one knee and heard something in the grass.

The corpse of The Rider stirred. His fingers flinched and curled, and with it, the sound of chainmail slowly ground together. He shifted his massive weight, and his legs curled. Then one by one, life was returned to each of his limbs, and he stirred himself afoot.

Argo watched in horror, petrified as the monster rose to his hands and knees and lifted himself back to his full stature. He was still facing away when he poised and collected himself. Then without moving a step, he reached over and slowly wrapped his hand around the hilt of his blade, which rested perfectly in his reach. In a quick and immediate motion, he drew the blade from the ground and whirled it in the moonlight. Its shadow danced dreadfully across Argo.

He sprang to his feet, nearly forgetting his sword. He reached down and grabbed it, almost dropping it again as he rose.

The Rider stood stoically faced away from him. He examined his blade in the moonlight and wiped away the mud, paying no attention to his assailant behind him. Once he was done, he lowered his sword and turned toward Argo.

The two now stood face-to-face again, swords drawn with only the moonlight and flowers between them.

Argo's heart raced wildly at the shock of the unexpected. The sight of the risen corpse filled him with helplessness, a certainty that there was nothing more he could do.

Finally, The Rider stepped forward and raised his sword again.

Argo made no move to shield himself. His entire body froze in terror, fully anticipating the final blow.

In one fluid motion, The Rider whirled the great blade again and slid it into his sheath. "Sit, Argo," he ordered.

Argo stood shaking, unsure of what he'd heard. He looked at The Rider with a confused expression.

"You heard me correctly. Sit, please." The Rider gestured to Argo, and then lowered himself to the ground, pulling up his sheathed sword so he could sit cross-legged in the grass.

Without question, Argo followed suit and sat in the same manner with his legs crossed.

The Rider lay his sword across the flowers in front of him. He faced Argo with perfect posture and rested his palms on his kneecaps. "Do you know why I let you win?" he asked in his deep, otherworldly tone.

Argo shook his head and wiped away tears, still in shock from the moment. He could hardly collect himself enough to speak. "No," he muttered.

"Your friend was watching." The Rider's words were crisp and articulate, and as he spoke, he almost felt human, even relatable.

"I don't know if I would call him my friend anymore," Argo responded.

"Do not be so quick to judge. His strength to enter these woods was very different from your own," The Rider explained.

Argo looked away bitterly, still swollen with his emotion. "He left me. And he threatened to kill Wander if I didn't go back with him."

"You may not have done the same because it is not in your nature to do so. Entering these woods was not in his nature, yet there he was," The Rider answered. "The courage of a man doomed to perish is very different from one who can still live."

Argo understood The Rider's words and felt embarrassed, like they were one more blow to his already muddy quest. He'd set off with only the best intentions to become a hero, yet each leg of the journey seemed only to dig at his blind ambition. Argo was beaten, muddied, swollen, ashamed, disappointed, and worst of all, hopeless.

"The reason I let you win, Argo, is because the world needs stories," The Rider explained.

"I feel like such a fool."

"Some may see it as such. Others may see it differently. It is not for us to decide how others view our stories. What is ours to decide is what we do in them."

Argo sat with his head in his hands. "What was I supposed to do?" he asked The Rider.

"Exactly what you did, Argo. You could have stayed in your village and waited for me, though that was never an option for you, was it?" The Rider asked.

Argo raised his head from his hands and looked at him. He shook his head quietly.

"You could have left the Hallowed Woods when it guided you back home, but you did not. You could have run from the beast and from Silas and even refused the ferryman, but you did not. Though you had choices, they were never options for you. The decisions you make are rooted deep within your character, so much so that the paths which appear to us only serve to remind us of who we really are."

Argo wiped away some of his remaining tears and looked aside and into the forest. "What does it matter if all my character did was lead me to become a fool?"

"A fool to whom? To your village? The ones who turned and held their own at the sword to stop you? If their advice meant nothing to you, why does their criticism?" he asked.

The point made by The Rider struck a chord within Argo. Why did he care what they thought? He cared about them as his people, though he never felt as though he was one of them. They cared nothing for him, and it hurt. They didn't send out Abaddon and Castor for his safety; they sent them out of fear for their own.

"You're right," Argo admitted. "How does this end?"

The Rider remained as stoic as ever. "You know how this ends."

Tears formed and swelled in the pit of Argo's eyes. "And Wander? Can she come with us?"

The Rider slowly turned and stared at the gentle animal wrapped in Argo's cloak, then turned back to face Argo once more. "Not like this."

Argo's stomach sank drastically. "I can't leave her. I can't let her die alone." He choked out the words and thought of her lying in the meadow all alone, afraid, abandoned.

"There is never a good time to leave," The Rider answered.

"She's dying. She's nearly there. She doesn't have any time left." He pleaded with tears in his eyes.

"Yet she lives," The Rider responded. "And we must go."

An excruciating sorrow fell upon Argo, as if the weight of the world suddenly bore down on him. He understood The Rider, and he looked at Wander still laboriously breathing under his cloak. In that instant, she was a puppy again, running with him through the Woods and chasing him through his cabin. She weaved around their furniture and around his father and around his mother's legs as she cooked their dinner.

He saw her chasing squirrels up trees and sleeping on her back in his bed. He saw her lying with his mother on their last night together and whining when she had to leave. He saw her bite his father's hand and run to him in the forest when no one else would follow. She fought against a murder of crows and played in and out of streams and slept with him on a pier. He remembered how he felt when she had fallen into the river and was found again, and how she lay on the deck with a broken paw. He saw all the times she looked at him.

And he cried.

Argo looked back at The Rider, who remained seated in front of him. He swallowed and cleared his throat, and without a single word, uncrossed his legs and stood up, reaching down only for his sword. The blade shone brightly in the moonlight as he approached her, still lying peacefully under his cloak.

He bent down and placed his forehead against hers. It was cold and wet, and her breath was strained and heavy. He scratched her behind her ears and kissed her where his head had lain. He tightened his grip around his sword, perfectly aligning one finger at a time, as he'd always practiced. Then he grabbed a corner of his cloak, cut a long wide strip from it, and carefully tied a loop at one end.

He wrapped the strip around his hand and shifted his position to behind Wander, who was still too tired to move. Argo's moonlit shadow fell across the cloak blanket and her black and brown fur. The cool breeze remained steadfast and the illuminated wildflowers brushed gently with it.

The night was clear now, and the stars above reminded him of the cave. Wander licked her stout slowly and closed her eyes again. He reached into his pack and pulled out the last bit of cheese, then held it in front of her. She smelled it, then softly lapped it up. Her tongue stuck slightly out of her mouth. Argo leaned down and gave her one more hug, slipping the thick cloth strip around her neck. He held her tightly.

"I love you, girl," he told her one last time before threading the running end through the loop. Quickly, he pulled the end tight and pressed his weight down against her. She kicked and bucked with a tenacious force, and still he pulled tightly with all his might, telling her it was going to be okay.

Wander fought with the little strength she had while he held her tightly. His head pressed against hers. "It's okay, girl, it's okay," he said calmly, feeling disconnected even from himself.

Memories of life together rushed through his mind like knives. Moments later, the beating ceased. Argo held his grip, still not ready to let go.

She was gone.

CHAPTER 37

The Rider's Bane

Argo rolled over beside Wander's lifeless body. His gut wrenched, and from deep within him, a loud, torturous cry bellowed out. His best friend was gone. He covered her body in his cloak.

Moments passed, then slowly he collected himself and rose weakly to his knees and feet.

The Rider and his mount watched solemnly. "The time is upon us," he said.

Argo stood over the cloak-covered remains of his best friend and nodded in understanding. He could barely muster the courage to respond. "Has been for some time now."

The Rider stood up in full strength and walked over to his mare, who was calmly eating some of the wildflowers. He petted her neck, opened the burlap sack, and reached deep inside, pulling out a fresh apple. He held it in front of her, and the horse swallowed it whole.

"There is an invisible thread that ties us together," The Rider said, "between a man and his fate." With his mighty hand, The Rider pushed aside his horse's armor, revealing a giant, ghastly scar running across his neck.

The Rider never turned back to face Argo. Instead, he stroked his heavy hand down the horse's mane as it continued chewing away.

Argo stared deeply at the discolored scar tissue. He had become disconnected from reality, left in some sort of free fall through space and time and connection—numb from the pain and the anguish and, most of all, from the long road. "I understand." Argo said softly. "Why you do it. I understand."

The Rider turned toward him.

Argo stood tall, holding out his meager sword.

"Come," he said, "you have suffered enough. I will not make you fight me."

"Please," Argo replied.

***

The Rider looked at Argo for a moment, almost unrecognizable from who he once was. "Your friend is no longer watching. It is only us who remain," The Rider explained.

"I know," Argo said calmly. He took his stance and extended his sword outward once more. Behind him, in a bed of wildflowers, lay his bundled cloak.

The Rider stood motionless and watched the young man. Then he stepped forward and drew his mighty blade.

The two swordsmen stood in the moonlit shadows of the meadow, and the gentle breeze blew between them.

Epilogue

The old man walked on crutches slowly to the center of the town square and sat carefully on a tree stump. The entire village had gathered around to listen to the old man's final tale. The night was cool and crisp, and above them shone a bright, full moon.

The old man cleared his throat and began in a voice so feeble that the entire circle closed in even tighter than before so that they, too, could hear. "I have told you the story of Argo and his faithful companion. You are all familiar with his journey and the places he went, the beings he met, the death of our beloved Castor, who bravely accompanied me on my quest, and how Argo was ultimately killed by the great hand of The Rider, as duty permitted."

The old man cleared his throat again and spoke laboriously. "You are all well aware that his father entered the Hallowed Woods on his own accord the morning I returned and was never seen again. After Argo's departure, the Lady of the Woods, wanted for her lies and mischief, was also never seen again, though it is believed she entered the Woods as well."

"As you know," he continued, "The Rider has not visited us since. Because of that, we have suffered immeasurable horrors. We have returned to natural deaths. Endured war, suffering, and lost many of our dear friends and family to the harsh realities of this world."

The old man paused in the emotion of the moment.

The entire crowd hung desperately in the suspenseful silence.

He looked up at the bright moon above and continued. "I'm here tonight to tell you that I have not been truthful." He choked up in shame and continued. "I was there. I watched from the cover of the Woods when Argo met The Rider. I watched the two clash in battle." He choked and then pressed on. "I watched Argo defeat The Rider. That night… I watched The Rider fall dead. And I ran."

The massive crowd broke out in a loud and chaotic gasp, whispering and then yelling to one another. Their cries drowned out the old man's voice.

The village officials yelled and did their best to calm the crowd and let the old man continue, which after several moments came to be.

He held his hands out in front of him. "I did not wish to tell you this out anger and resentment towards you all, the village which sent Castor and I to hunt down our friend. I wanted you to believe that The Rider abandoned us because of our shameful reaction to Argo's quest. Alas, I'm at the end of my days, and I have lived with this truth every day since. Argo succeeded in his quest. He was truly brave." The old man stood.

Again, the crowd roared with fury, arguing among one another and beating against the town officials, who desperately held them back from attacking the old man. Slowly, he turned away from them and looked down the path to the Hallowed Woods.

He reached into his pocket one last time and pulled out a letter. It was the first to come since his return many years ago. He slowly limped on his cane down the path and away from the mob, leaving the raging upset and chaos behind him. The path was overgrown and untrodden, and remnants of it barely remained. Yet he knew where it lay because he had dreamed of it every lonesome day for all those years since his return.

He reached the end, where the trail used to fade into grass—where he, Castor, and their dear friend Emeric had once stood with Argo and his faithful companion Wander.

The crowd finally broke through the meager attempts to hold them back and were tearing down the trail toward the old man. The torches held in their one hand outlined the spears in their other.

Abaddon looked to the stars and moon above as he stood shamefully at the edge of the tree line.

Out of the forest to meet him walked a man and his dog. Her tail wagged happily.

THE RIDER'S BANE

About the Author

Jacob Acebo is a proud Texan born and raised in Corpus Christi where he grew up playing videogames, surfing, and causing mayhem outdoors. He holds a degree in Psychology from Texas A&M University, where he participated as a member Company K-2 in the Corps of Cadets and the Texas A&M Recon Company. It was a debaucherously great time of growth, unfettered masculinity, and low grades.

After graduation in 2015, Jacob commissioned in the United States Marine Corps and was stationed in Kaneohe Bay, Hawaii where he served two deployments as an Infantry Officer before earning the title of Reconnaissance Marine. In 2021, after six years of unforgettable friends, Hawaiian sunsets, and unbelievable surf, he left the military to return to his home in Texas.

Today, Jacob resides in Georgetown, TX and is working towards his MBA at St. Edward's University. In his free time, he shares his love for hunting, fishing, and the outdoors through his Instagram account, @SilentStagChronicles. He is a proud father of two dogs, Luna, who served as the inspiration for Wander, and a puppy rightfully named Argos. Passionate about great stories which inspire us to become better, Jacob Acebo is excited to share his debut novel with the world.

www.ingramcontent.com/pod-product-compliance
Lightning Source LLC
Chambersburg PA
CBHW031529310726
48971CB00008B/2409